THE KING OF LIGHTING FIXTURES

Camino del Sol

A Latina and Latino Literary Series

THE KING OF LIGHTING FIXTURES

STORIES

DANIEL A. OLIVAS

THE UNIVERSITY OF
ARIZONA PRESS
TUCSON

The University of Arizona Press
www.uapress.arizona.edu

Printed in the United States of America
22   21   20   19   18   17   6   5   4   3   2   1

ISBN-13: 978-0-8165-3562-0 (paper)

Cover design by Leigh McDonald
Cover art: *El rey de la risa* by Eloy Torrez

The epigraph on p. vii is from "The 10 Commandments of Writing About L.A." by Daniel Olivas, *Los Angeles Magazine*, December 2015.

Publication of this book is made possible in part by the proceeds of a permanent endowment created with the assistance of a Challenge Grant from the National Endowment for the Humanities, a federal agency.

Library of Congress Cataloging-in-Publication Data
Names: Olivas, Daniel A., author.
Title: The king of lighting fixtures : stories / Daniel A. Olivas.
Other titles: Camino del sol.
Description: Tucson : The University of Arizona Press, 2017. | Series: Camino del sol : a Latina and Latino literary series.
Identifiers: LCCN 2016051179 | ISBN 9780816535620 (pbk. : alk. paper)
Subjects: LCSH: Mexican Americans—California—Los Angeles—Fiction. | LCGFT: Short stories.
Classification: LCC PS3615.L58 A6 2017 | DDC 813/.6—dc23 LC record available at https://lccn.loc.gov/2016051179

♾ This paper meets the requirements of ANSI/NISO Z39.48-1992 (Permanence of Paper).

For Sue and Ben:

You are my life, joy, and inspiration.

Los Angeles is in my bones; its streets course through my stories.
I keep nostalgia at bay: My L.A. roadways are gritty and crowded,
no room for celluloid dreams.

Contents

THE KING OF LIGHTING FIXTURES

Good Things Happen at Tina's Café

During waking hours, Félix José Costa would never allow himself to wonder how different life would be if he were just like everyone else. Average. Common. *Normal.* In that way he was quite wise despite his relative youth. Even at twenty-six years of age, Félix knew that it was a fool's destiny to expend energy imagining something that could never be.

But in his dreams—oh, those dreams!—he was like everyone else. In his nocturnal visions, Félix would saunter into the Ronald Reagan State Building's entrance on Spring Street and wave to the security guard, a heavyset, middle-aged man who would smile for no one but Félix. *Good morning! How about those Lakers!* And then a manly fist bump, another wave, a jaunty nod from both men. He'd then stroll along to the elevators waving to friends and colleagues, right hand (and sometimes his left) happily and publicly displayed for all to see, another beautiful day in Los Angeles, this grand City of Angels, Lotusland, a magical metropolis where dreams come true.

Compare reality: five mornings a week, after enjoying a cup or two of coffee at a nearby café, Félix enters his building, faux leather briefcase slung over his right shoulder, both hands jammed into his pants pockets, a slight turn to the guard so that he can see Félix's California-issued, laminated identification card clipped to his jacket pocket, a silent dance without emotion, and then on toward the elevators, averting his eyes from passersby. He eventually gets to the eleventh floor, finds his barren cubicle, and begins his day as a legal secretary for three deputy attorneys general and one paralegal, employees in the Public Rights Division of the California Department of Justice.

Félix had learned the word for his "circumstance" when he was relatively young. His mother, Josefina, being quite educated and unafraid of reality, believed in truth regardless of where it might lead one, even with regard to her only child. A day after Félix's sixth birthday—after a short life filled with

mockery and vicious jibes from neighborhood children and classmates—
Josefina wrote the word on a piece of scrap paper and had Félix find it in the
family's well-worn *American Heritage Dictionary*. Félix was very good with
words and loved the musty smell of the dictionary. He flipped the pages
until he came to the word his mother had written down: "pol-y-dac-tyl
(pŏl'ē-dăk'təl) *adj.* Having more than the normal number of fingers or toes."

Félix rested his right hand on the page, palm on the cool, smooth paper,
six fingers spread wide. There was *that* word: "normal." And he sighed. But
Josefina swelled with pride because Félix pronounced it correctly. What a
talented boy! What a handsome, promising, smart boy!

Félix's father, Reymundo, was not as educated as Josefina. No, he was a
man of the old ways. His son was cursed. Period. And the only way to fight
a curse was through magic. One week after Félix learned the word for his
condition, and unbeknownst to his wife, Reymundo took his son to visit a
childless widower cousin named Tony who lived south of Koreatown on
Ardmore Avenue near 15th Street in a rambling, two-story, wood-frame
house built circa 1910 that was excessively large for Tony. But too many
memories kept him in his home. Tony had what people called a sunny
disposition, a man who never complained but spent his days appreciating
the little things in life. He stayed put, thanked the heavens for his abode,
for the many years he had spent with his late, lovely wife, Trini, and lived
alone with his memories.

Nevertheless, Tony knew others suffered from loss, and he possessed
a gift that could help them. Put simply, he could do wondrous things with
mud and a few primordial incantations. For example, if your husband
of fifty years finally succumbed to that undetected anomalous coronary
artery, Tony could make a new spouse for you, complete with that little
paunch and a more or less working male anatomy, out of the deep-brown
mud from his backyard. Your beloved beagle got hit by a car? Presto-
change-o! A new canine with the same sweet disposition and memories
. . . expertly shaped by Tony's elegant, long fingers out of mud. And Tony
offered his talents at a bargain, too! If you were hard up, he'd take payment
in house cleaning, tree trimming, or home-cooked pork tamales. People
said that Tony was a saint. One would be hard put to argue with such an
assessment. But when some asked Tony why he didn't make a muddy
double of his late wife, Tony would only wave the question away, shake his
head, and say: "Not possible." This response could have several meanings.
Some thought that he would lose his gift if he selfishly used it for himself.

Others believed that Tony idolized Trini so much that he didn't know if he could do her justice with simple mud. Regardless, Tony's friends, family, and neighbors appreciated what he did for them, and that was that.

So, one bright Saturday morning, Reymundo told Josefina that he was going to take Félix to hike at Griffith Park knowing full well that his beautiful, brilliant wife did not like to perspire in public. She wished them well. Though the west San Fernando Valley had more than its share of trails that snaked up into the Santa Monica Mountains, Griffith Park sat at the eastern end of that same mountain range and boasted other attractions such as an observatory and planetarium, not to mention the nearby zoo, the Autry National Center, and the Greek Theatre. Reymundo and Félix kissed Josefina goodbye, hopped in the Honda Civic, and left Canoga Park for nature. But they took a detour to visit Tony, who lived just a few miles from their final destination. Though Félix was puzzled when his father stayed on the 101 instead of switching over to the 134, he kept quiet and simply enjoyed the ride. When they exited at Normandie Avenue, Félix knew where his father was taking him. After a few minutes they parked in front of Tony's house. Félix figured his father needed to chat with his cousin for a few moments just to see how he was getting along in that big, empty house.

But no. Félix's father clearly had other plans. Tony came out to greet them, hands and arms covered in dark mud. Despite his equally muddy Levi's and red T-shirt, Tony could not hide his innate elegance. He had a head full of white, curly hair, a countenance made up of sharp, regal features. Tony could have been an actor, everyone said, but he loved his magic too much to think of such silliness.

"Vámonos," he said through a broad smile. "Follow me to the backyard. I don't want to hug you two since, as you can see, I am a muddy mess."

Tony's yard was immense, a double lot with a massive old avocado tree at its center. A grassy lawn covered most of the yard. Here and there were a few small lemon trees, a rose bush or two. Félix's eyes were drawn to Tony's shed at the far end of the yard, just to the left of a thick cover of morning glory vines that twined in and out of the chain-link fence that separated Tony's property from a well-maintained fourplex apartment building. Hundreds of flowers had just opened fully to display trumpets of vibrant blues and purples dappled with morning dew. To the right of the vines was a vast, wet pit of mud that was clearly the source of Tony's medium of choice.

Tony walked toward the shed as his guests followed. When they entered, Tony clicked on the overhead fluorescent lights and stopped. The loamy smell overtook Félix for a moment making him blink and then sneeze. He had never been invited into his cousin's workspace before.

"Come in," Tony said. He pointed to an ancient blue velvet couch and nodded to Reymundo, who obeyed the silent command to sit.

"Un momento . . . I have little more preparation to take care of," said Tony as he walked to his workbench where a wet pile of mud sat waiting. "Make yourself at home," and he turned to the mud, plunged his hands into it, and started to hum a nondescript little tune.

Félix stood still and scanned the sparsely furnished room. Other than the couch, a lone metal folding chair stood in one corner. A muddy white towel hung from a large nail in the wall behind the workbench. Above his father's head was a single wooden bookshelf attached precariously to the wall. Félix could make out a few of the titles. *Sculpture of Africa* by Eliot Elisofon. Paulo Freire's *Pedagogy of the Oppressed*. *Aztec Thought and Culture* by Miguel León-Portillo. He squinted to discern what other books sat on the shelf but could only make out two that had the word "wrestling" in the titles. Félix's mother said that despite Tony's belief in magic, he was quite an intellectual who read two or three books a week on everything from art to philosophy to history. His reading material seemed to support this. Tony also seemed to enjoy the art of wrestling, and judging from the tight ropes of muscle that undulated in his shoulders and arms while he worked the mud, Tony very likely had wrestled in his younger years. Félix had tried to watch a wrestling match during the last Summer Olympics, but he found it boring and nothing like he thought wrestling should be like. The two men almost never touched each other and looked like two cats prancing on their hind legs. Yet the Cuban won the gold over the American. How? Why?

"Estoy listo," said Tony.

Félix jumped just a bit and turned to the workbench. Tony stood to the side of the mud, which he had sculpted into the shape of a small sheet cake. Félix walked slowly toward Tony, who offered a welcoming smile. Finally, the boy stood in front of the workbench and looked down and saw what Tony had been doing: in the mud were two perfectly formed imprints of five-fingered hands. Félix's stomach leapt.

"No tengas miedo," whispered Tony. "It won't hurt. Just fit your hands into the mud, palms down."

"But . . ."

Tony understood: "Fit your two outside fingers into the pinkies . . . the mud will give just a bit because it's still wet."

Félix turned his head to his father, who now sat at the edge of the couch, elbows resting on his knees, hands folded as if in prayer. He nodded to Félix.

The boy turned toward the workbench and slowly placed his hands into the mud. It felt cool, moist, almost comforting.

"¡Excelente!" exclaimed Tony as he scooped up fresh mud and covered Félix's hands. When Tony finished, he stepped back and admired his work. He then closed his eyes and mumbled something in a language Félix did not recognize.

"Now what?" asked Reymundo.

Tony's eyes popped open. "Now," he said as he reached for the towel, "you and I will go and have a beer in the house while the boy stands here for an hour."

"What?" said Félix unable to hide his alarm.

Tony smiled: "Do you think that great magic can happen in a minute?"

Of course, this made sense. Félix sighed, nodded, and closed his eyes.

"Good boy," said Tony. "Reymundo, I have some cold Buds in the fridge. Let's go."

Reymundo stood and walked to his son. He kissed Félix on the top of his head and inhaled the perspiration that permeated his son's thick hair. Reymundo loved his son deeply and just wanted to make Félix's life a little easier. After a few moments, Reymundo lifted his head and looked down at the muddy magic.

"It'll be over soon," he offered as Tony started to lead him toward the door. "You are a brave young man."

Félix kept his eyes closed, falling into what his mother called a self-induced trance, something the boy had mastered when he needed to escape this world. An hour later the sound of Tony's cheerful voice brought him back to this world.

"Let's see those hands of yours."

Félix's father stood to the side. Tony opened a battered tool chest that sat on the workbench, reached in, and pulled out a mud-stained wooden stick that resembled a large, broken spoon. With the sharp end he slowly chiseled away the now-dried mud. Tony and his father affixed their eyes on the stick and followed it as Tony uncovered first the thumbs, moving outward toward the offending extra digits. When he finally finished, Félix held up his hands and wiggled his fingers.

Six fingers on each hand. Félix sighed.

Tony turned to Reymundo. "Have you explored surgery?"

"The insurance won't cover the procedure, and it's so expensive."

Tony asked, "How could they not cover it?"

"Look," said Reymundo. "All of his fingers work perfectly. So they consider it merely cosmetic surgery. Elective."

"Pendejos," muttered Tony.

———————————

Twenty years later, Tony was three years dead and his favorite cousin, Félix, now lived in the big house. And one Thursday morning, after catching the bus at Pico and Ardmore, Félix sat at Tina's Café enjoying a delicious cup of Yuban and reading the *Times* a half hour before the workday began. His twelve fingers wrapped around the coffee mug. He felt so at home here. The other customers were not professionals but men and women who had little money and even less hope of improving their lives. Not one of them ever stared at his hands. All offered a smile and a nod, nothing more. But that was quite a gift as far as Félix was concerned.

He had discovered Tina's Café while searching Yelp for places near his office. He was intrigued by its lone three-star review by a person named Barney whose photo revealed the inscrutable countenance of a young, slightly dazed-looking, unkempt man:

> Located at 357 1/2 S. Spring Street. Founded in 2008, Tina's Café has nurtured a loyal following with its dedication to traditional coffee brands such as Folgers and Yuban. Convenient location with some of the lowest coffee prices in town. Decor has a garage sale feel to it, and the lighting could be improved, but the seating is comfortable and encourages random conversations. Unfortunately, the service is poor: Owner is often distant and seems preoccupied with some other venture, but this might be an act. Also, customers must clean up after themselves or else the owner gets very cross and points a finger at the offending mess. Even so, a much better deal than the nearby Third Street Deli.

Félix had tried to speak with Tina the first time he came in a year ago, but true to the Yelp review, she was not responsive. She was content to pour coffee and collect money. Was she pretty? Maybe. Young? Not certain. Félix suspected that Tina was about five years older than he, but then again, she could be two or three years younger. Was she Mexican? Probably not. Maybe she was Filipina or perhaps Native American. She did not engage any customer in conversation. Tina was Tina, and that was that.

But on this Thursday morning, after Tina poured Félix a second cup of coffee, she didn't turn to attend to other customers but, rather, stood before Félix and waited for something.

Félix looked up and tried to smile, but his face wouldn't comply. Tina's face remained passive as she stared into his eyes.

"Yes?" Félix finally said.

"You have six fingers on each hand, you know."

"Yes, I know."

"Good," said Tina before turning away. "Glad you know it."

The next morning, after Tina poured Félix's first cup of coffee she said, "I have three breasts."

Félix almost fell out of his chair. Tina laughed.

"Not really," she said. "I just made that up."

Félix looked down at the tabletop and put his hands in his lap, out of sight.

"But," continued Tina now that the dam was broken, "I'm sure there are women out there, someplace, who do have three breasts, don't you think?"

Félix nodded.

Tina pulled up a chair, sat down with a little grunt, and put the coffee pot down on the table.

"Women just love those hands, don't they?"

Félix looked up at the clock on the wall, pulled out three dollars, dropped them on the table, and stood.

"Going to be late for work," he said but didn't move.

"No, you're not," said Tina. "You always leave here at eight fifteen. It's only seven fifty. Sit. You have time. I won't bother you anymore."

As Félix took his seat again, Tina stood and walked to another customer. A minute later, she came back to his table.

"I'm sorry," she said. "I was being rude. I have no right to ask such questions, right?"

"Not a big deal," said Félix. For reasons he could not understand, he hoped she'd sit down again.

"Saturday morning," she began, "I think we should meet at the base of Angels Flight. Then we can figure out what to do for the day."

Before he could stop himself, Félix said, "I'd like that."

"Groovy," said Tina. She finally smiled. "Let's make it ten in the a.m., as my papa would say."

"Ten in the a.m.," he said. "It's a date."

"You bet it is," said Tina. "There's nothing else you could call it even if you tried."

Félix stood at the base of Angels Flight on Hill Street. He was seven minutes early, so he walked back and forth and occasionally looked up at the two orange-and-black funicular cars as they clacked up and down the parallel tracks. Félix looked at the time on his iPhone. Five more minutes. He noticed a small plaque and took three steps, leaned close, and read it:

> Built in 1901 by Colonel J. W. Eddy, lawyer, engineer, and friend of President Lincoln, Angels Flight is said to be the world's shortest incorporated railway. The counterbalanced cars, controlled by cables, travel a 33 percent grade for 315 feet. It is estimated that Angels Flight has carried more passengers per mile than any other railway in the world, over a hundred million in its first fifty years. This incline railway is a public utility operating under a franchise granted by the City of Los Angeles.

"You know they have names."

Félix tried not to show his surprise but failed. He looked up into the morning sun and squinted into Tina's shadowed face. "What?"

"Sinai and Olivet," said Tina. "That's their names."

"Who?"

"The cars, silly."

"Oh," said Félix. "Why?"

"Biblical, of course."

"Of course."

Tina held out her right hand, palm up. At first, Félix thought she wanted to hold his hand, but then noticed that she presented four shiny quarters.

"Our funicular fare," said Tina. "We pay the kind gentleman at the top. Fifty cents per person each way."

"I know."

"Oh, you are a wise and experienced man."

Félix blushed and turned away.

"Let's go," she said. "Time is *not* on our side."

When they got to the top and paid their fare, Tina said: "Must. Drink. Coffee."

"There's a Starbucks right over there."

"Starbucks is evil," she said. "Starbucks was created to destroy small business people like me."

"Oh, sorry," said Félix. "Of course you believe that."

"Yes, you should be ashamed of yourself."

"I am."

"Good," said Tina as she started to walk toward the Starbucks. "Let's go to Starbucks."

Félix didn't move. "What?"

"Starbucks is evil but I have a hankerin' for a Caffè Vanilla Frappuccino Blended Coffee."

Félix took a step and then another after Tina. "That sounds good."

"Yes, it's delicious," she said with a smack of her lips. "And then we'll sit and talk for a bit about very important things and go to MOCA, which opens at eleven, to look at an exhibit or two or three and then come back here and grab some Panda Express since I am already now craving orange chicken for lunch and we can talk about less important things and then we'll take Angels Flight back down and find a bar or two or three and have a microbrew or some fancy girl's drink and then find some other places to hang out because we are young and the day lies before us like a cornucopia filled with unforgettable and life-changing experiences."

Félix smiled.

"It does appear that you like my plan," said Tina.

"I think I do."

Tina stopped walking to let Félix catch up to her. "I repeat: you are a wise and experienced man," she said when he finally stood by her side.

"I guess I am," he said. "I guess I am."

And they spent the day more or less as Tina had planned, though it was Félix's idea to walk to Olvera Street to eat dinner at La Golondrina Mexican Café. They spoke of many things, whatever came into their heads, as the hours passed.

For example, at 10:31 a.m. over their blended Starbucks coffee drinks, Tina said: "You know, George Bernard Shaw wrote a scathing review of Brahms, called him a 'great baby' and said that he was 'addicted to dressing himself up as Handel or Beethoven and making a prolonged and intolerable noise.' Can you imagine? Brahms? A 'great baby'? Craziness!"

And at 12:57 p.m. as they stood in line at Panda Express, Félix said: "Did you know that Panda Express Executive Chef Andy Kao is widely considered the creator of orange chicken? And they sold over sixty million pounds of it last year? Amazing."

And it was precisely 2:13 p.m. as they rode Sinai back down to Hill Street that Tina offered this: "Wilshire Boulevard was named after Henry Gaylord Wilshire, who was from Cincinnati and was known as a bit of a flirt and a definite rabble-rouser. At least that's what I read in a book by this guy named Kevin Roderick."

It was 6:39 p.m. as they strolled along Olvera Street toward La Golondrina for dinner when they said absolutely nothing—not a peep—which was just fine by them.

Their day ended at 10:03 p.m. at the base of Angels Flight, just where it had started. They stood facing each other, swaying in the cool evening, bellies full, heads a bit woozy from microbrews and lady drinks.

"One kiss?" asked Félix.

"One kiss it is," said Tina.

And they kissed, bodies apart, faces turned in, lips tentative, a flicker of tongue. After a few moments, they pulled back in unison.

"I assume you will come by the very famous Tina's Café on Monday morning," said Tina.

"I'll be there," said Félix.

"I know you will," said Tina.

And they went their separate ways.

It was a foggy Monday morning as Félix stepped off the bus and walked toward Spring Street. He had had all of Sunday to think about his day with

Tina. The chilled air allowed him to see his breath. Félix tried not to smile, but he couldn't help himself. He would soon be in Tina's Café having a hot cup of Yuban poured by Tina herself.

Félix walked past a storefront with its name, *Mike's Used Furniture*, in old-fashioned, golden script emblazoned across the plate glass. Below the name was: *Est'd. 1962*. He stopped and walked back. He looked up at the address: 357 1/2 South Spring Street. The lights were out, the store not yet open for business. Félix pulled his hands from his jacket pockets and cupped his eyes so that he could look into the store. He leaned forward and squinted. Instead of Tina's Café, he saw bureaus and chairs and tables and loveseats neatly arranged and ready for sale.

Félix pulled back, placed his palms onto the plate glass, unable to catch his breath. He closed his eyes and tried to conjure Tina's face in his mind's eye, but couldn't. His legs began to buckle and it took every bit of concentration to avoid falling down onto the cold sidewalk. After a full minute, Félix opened his eyes and focused on his splayed fingers. He blinked once and then again and then once more. Five. *Five!* Five fingers on each hand. He brought his hands away from the plate glass, turned toward the street, mouth open like an empty wallet. And at that moment every memory of Tina slipped from his mind.

He closed his mouth into a tight smile. And with a little laugh, Félix José Costa raised his perfectly normal hands into the cool Los Angeles morning.

Juana

Juana told me to meet her at El Museo de Arte Moderno. Right by *The Two Fridas* at noon she said. Juana knew that I despised Frida Kahlo's obsession with herself and that it would have been just as easy for us to get together at the Colón Misión Reforma where she's staying. And she also knew that she would arouse my suspicions by keeping me away from her hotel. But she always liked to tweak me, get my goat as they say in the United States. I couldn't refuse Juana, of course. And she knew that, too.

It'd rained all morning but mercifully stopped just before I went out to flag down a taxi. The sky remained gray and oppressive as honking cars and buses strangled the slick streets. I've found that my ability to remain calm in Mexico City's traffic, especially when it rains, has seeped away with each year so that I'd rather spend a few pesos for someone else to sweat through it for me. Though I'd left plenty of time, it took too long to get there. I gave my driver a generous tip and then remembered that I'd have to pay the museum's admission fee, which annoyed me further. It figured that there'd be a charge to see Juana.

After buying a ticket, I entered the museum and approached the information desk to ask where I would find *The Two Fridas*. The woman offered a smile that let me know two things. First, she didn't mind the way I looked in my dark blue suit. Second, she was proud to direct me to one of the museum's most appreciated pieces. I nodded my thanks and returned her smile. If things didn't work out with Juana, I figured I could pay another visit to the information desk.

I got to the painting but Juana wasn't there. I glanced at my watch. I was no more than five minutes late. But certainly even Juana wouldn't force someone, especially her ex-husband, to meet her at a museum and then leave because of a mere five minutes. A tour group of about seven Americans stood too close to the Kahlo painting as the guide explained each symbolic element. He called the canvas a masterpiece of self-awareness. I call it nothing more than solipsism.

"Magnificent, isn't it?"

I turned. Juana stood not more than a foot behind me, arms crossed, head cocked to the right, pretending to admire the painting.

"Un pedazo de mierda," I said, even though Juana had made her pronouncement in English.

The tour guide stopped in mid-sentence. Luckily the Americans didn't seem to understand what I'd said. I turned to the guide, offered an apologetic shrug, and tried to lead Juana away. She wouldn't move.

"Not even a kiss hello?" she asked still speaking in English.

She wanted to annoy me as much as possible, but I wouldn't let her win. My English was as good as hers so I jumped right in.

"But of course," I said as I leaned in and kissed her cheek. She smelled of cigarettes, perspiration, and a perfume she'd never worn while we were married.

"Much better," Juana whispered. "Where can we talk?"

I scanned the area and spied a free bench by a large Rufino Tamayo canvas. We made our way to it and sat. We looked at each other for a minute or so in silence. I figured Juana should begin since she was the one who had flown to Mexico City to see me.

"I need help," she finally said.

"I figured as much."

Juana snorted and turned away from me. Her eyes rested on the Tamayo. I looked at her left hand and grew excited. Her ring finger sported nothing more than a pale line. Could she have left Reynaldo already? Sure. Why not? I never expected them to last. Two ex-husbands before Juana reached twenty-five.

"Did I waste my time coming home?" she said keeping her eyes from mine.

"I thought Los Angeles was home now."

Juana turned to me. I tried to read her eyes the way I used to, but I couldn't. As my curiosity started to swirl and gain momentum, Juana touched my hand. Actually, not quite a touch. She put her hand just above mine so that I could feel the heat from her palm. But she never really made contact with my skin.

"Let's go," she said. "Vamos al hotel."

As I lay in bed, I rested my eyes on the large and sole window in Juana's hotel room. It'd started raining again on the way here but the sun was now beginning to peek out from behind the clouds. My stomach rumbled because Juana preferred to make love rather than eat lunch. While we were married, she often made me delay my meals on the theory that a hungry body could feel more sensation. I never believed it. And now as she snored softly next to me, I fantasized about gorging myself on succulent carnitas and steaming corn tortillas washed down with cup after cup of hot, black coffee. Juana stirred and before I knew it her eyes were wide open, staring at me. I reached over and touched her face. She didn't respond.

"Él está muerto," she announced without a flinch.

I sat up, confused. "Who's dead?"

"Reynaldo."

"How?"

Juana got out of bed. She wore only a large T-shirt that made her look even tinier than she was. She folded her arms and paced back and forth on the red shag carpet. This room had been elegant once, but now it looked a bit frayed at the edges, unstylish, out of a different era.

"I had left him a few months ago," she said, keeping her eyes on her feet as they moved. "But he wanted to see me, to talk."

I nodded, understanding what Reynaldo had felt.

"And?"

"And so he cooked dinner for me," said Juana. "Halibut."

I didn't need to know what they ate. But I let her continue.

"We were having a good time, really. It was fine to talk. And then it happened."

"What?"

Juana stopped pacing, dropped her arms and stared at me. "Reynaldo started choking, on a bone."

Ah, that's why she mentioned the halibut. But I was still confused.

"So they couldn't save him from a fish bone?"

Her left eye twitched. And then I understood what she was trying to say.

"You didn't call for help, did you?" I said.

Juana didn't answer but she didn't have to.

"When was the funeral?"

She shook her head.

"Juana," I said. "When was the funeral?"

She walked to the bed, lifted the covers, and snuggled next to me. I sank into the mattress and pulled her close.

"He's still there," said Juana. "In his house."

At that moment I probably should have jumped out of bed to get away from her. But I didn't. Instead, I pulled Juana closer.

"When did it happen?" I asked using a tone that would've been appropriate to ask a young child where she had lost her favorite doll. Juana didn't answer, as if she had to think about it.

"What day is it?" she finally asked me.

"Sunday."

"Sunday?"

"Yes."

Juana exhaled loudly through her mouth. I felt a hot tear fall onto my chest.

"Monday," she said.

I turned away and looked at the window. The sky grew brighter as the clouds continued to dissipate. Juana's breathing grew heavy.

"Mi amor," I said softly.

She didn't answer. Within a few moments she snored softly into my chest. I kissed her hair and thought for a minute. I then carefully extricated myself from her body and dressed as quietly as I could. Before I left, I kissed Juana's forehead and touched her hair. As I reached the street, the sun shone brightly without obstruction for the first time all day. I waved down a taxi and got in.

"El Museo de Arte Moderno," I said without thinking.

The driver nodded and eased his car into traffic.

"Finally, some sun," he said as he caught my eye in the rearview mirror.

"Yes," I answered with a smile. "Finally."

Bar 107

If you've been wondering where I've been these last three years, let me just tell you right now that you can find me at Bar 107 downtown on Fourth Street most nights with a sheaf of paper—my unfinished novel—red Sharpie in hand, a glass of Pabst Blue Ribbon by my side for inspiration.

I've been editing the same first chapter for, well, three years. I didn't make tenure, something you'd know if you've been talking to Mónica, which would kind of surprise me since she was the ostensible reason for us breaking up when she and I got very drunk—right here at Bar 107— and you caught us messing around in that booth over there. I still think you overreacted since we did not go beyond what you can do in a booth in plain view—of course!—but you did come close enough to see that I had my left hand up her short skirt and inside her little black panties. I haven't seen her since that night. But I admit that when you moved out of my condo the next day, I texted her, tried to get *that* ball rolling, so to speak. I mean, Mónica is hot. You know that. Not as hot as you, but hot nonetheless. But she never responded, which makes me suspect she chose you over me and probably begged to remain your best friend.

I like Bar 107 for a few reasons including the fact that it's a short walk from the Pershing Square Station, which is important ever since I lost my car—well, it was repossessed—and lost my job and had to downsize my life in many annoying ways including selling the condo and then renting a one-bedroom in Koreatown. I'm not on unemployment anymore since I've managed to patch together a living by taking on a few private students and teaching creative writing online extension courses through UCLA. I mean, I *do* have an award-winning short-story collection to my name and have published in some of the better literary journals including *Tin House, Prairie Schooner, Huizache,* and *ZYZZYVA* to name but a few (I am not bragging . . . I'm simply stating the truth). That little fiction collection kept me legit for five full years, but my drinking and my cockiness and my writer's block all conspired to derail my pathway to tenure at the UNIVERSITY-THAT-SHALL-NOT-BE-NAMED. You'd think they'd never met an alcoholic writer for God's sake. Though I do suspect that the second complaint lodged against me by that perky little sophomore (who also shall not be named) didn't help. I mean, if she didn't want to be around me and my hands why didn't she just drop the class? Young people today, they have no sense of logic. If something bothers me, I walk away. That's how it's done. You don't have to ask me twice before I exit, stage right.

Anyway, my meager living doesn't keep me from Bar 107. I've actually made some great editing decisions right here. I think I've finally figured out how to begin this novel—writing the first chapter, getting it perfect, is what I have to do because that will set the stage for the rest of it—and once I get these first pages just so, the other chapters will flow like, well, Pabst Blue Ribbon from the tap. But if you do come by Bar 107 and see me hunched over my pages, wait until I take a break before coming by to say hi. I don't want anything to break the magic, not even you. You know how delicate the creative writing process is, right? I mean, you saw it up close and personal for long enough. Just be patient. I'll look up from my writing eventually. Really. I promise.

Mateo's Walk

Though he just celebrated his fiftieth birthday, Mateo refuses to give up his search. He knows that Isabel lives someplace near downtown Los Angeles, no doubt on a street Mateo has walked maybe a thousand times. And though it has been more than twenty years since they last saw each other, Mateo trusts his sharp eyes, eyes he inherited from his mother, eyes that could spot a jackrabbit in the hilly scrub near their small village in Mexico, his home from long ago. So, six mornings a week, Mateo puts on his baseball cap, slings a backpack onto his round shoulders, and walks ten blocks to work in the toy district, where he unpacks boxes, sweeps the floor, and sometimes acts as the cashier when Mrs. Kim needs to get lunch or take care of other business. This job is safe, simple, and keeps Mateo free to walk and search and dream. Today he takes a different route to work, different from the route he took yesterday, and the day before. Mateo knows he must alternate his trips so that he can increase the odds of finding Isabel. The morning is hot already, almost eighty degrees, the Santa Anas—the Devil Winds—spreading their evil. It is not a lucky day. But Mateo remains hopeful, trudging along Spring Street, perspiration covering his face like a thin veil, wishing he had left his jacket at home today. He turns left on Fourth Street. A man steps out of Bar 107 hugging a sheaf of papers to his chest, walks past Mateo, gives Mateo a nod, a smile. Mateo nods and smiles and continues. The people are so nice here in downtown, he thinks. Suddenly, for some reason, Mateo stops in front of a café and looks through the plate glass window. Why he stops here he does not know. He squints and eventually lets his gaze rest upon an empty table, a newspaper spread across it. Mateo wonders if Isabel had been sitting at that table, looking at the want ads or maybe looking for sales, and then perhaps she had just stood up for a second to use the restroom. He waits. One minute. Two, three. But no one comes back to the table. Not Isabel, not anyone else. Mateo exhales loudly. He turns and looks down

Fourth Street. It is time to get to work, he thinks. Mateo takes a step, and then another, picking up speed as he walks without thinking. He decides to take Third Street tomorrow. Yes, Mateo hasn't walked that street in a few days. Maybe tomorrow he will be lucky.

The Subtenant

I realize now that taking him on as my subtenant was not the wisest decision I ever made, setting aside my dating life, which could properly and without exaggeration be characterized as a decade-long disgrace. It's not that I suffered lasting damage to my apartment or my body. But I now have a certain image burned onto my memory that I wish I'd never acquired. Live and learn, my father would say. If he were still alive. My father was an idiot.

It's been a bit more than three years now since Satan first sent me an e-mail response to my Craigslist posting. Alarms should have gone off in my puny brain. I mean, who has an e-mail address like redboy666@aol.com? Redboy? AOL? But I hadn't had much luck with the ad, and I was kind of low on money since losing my paralegal job when the law firm downsized as the economy went down the shithole. I had some savings and picked up a little work here and there from this solo practitioner in Westwood, so I wasn't starving. But I needed an additional revenue flow, like right now.

When he showed up to look at my spare room and the pretty large bathroom that I was willing to share, I should have slammed the door on him the moment my brain fully comprehended what my eyes perceived. He was so pathetic, standing there on my *WELCOME!* mat, one large, raggedy suitcase resting by his cloven hooves, pointy tail drooping like a limp dick, horns dull and worn down to nubs. Sad. Contemptible. Wretched. But I guess that's why I let him in. He was in worse shape than I was.

So I showed Satan the spare bedroom, which he liked, made him smile just a bit. And when he saw the bathroom with its original pink-and-green midcentury tile and immaculate porcelain tub (all in mint condition, I might add), it was as if he were a little boy on Christmas day opening up the largest package under the tree. I have to admit my apartment is pretty great, which is why I've been here going on ten years now. Anyway, he yelped, I'll take it! It's perfect! Don't you want to see the kitchen? I asked. Nope, no need, he smiled. It's exactly what I need!

He could see that I hesitated so he pulled out a wad of hundreds (from I don't know where since he wasn't wearing any pants over his goat legs) and counted out the first and last months' rent and the security deposit. I was going to ask him how he knew the amount but I realized that was a stupid question. He held the money before me, fanning my face with the crisp bills. My mouth started to water. What to do? What to do? Well, I grabbed the money, shook his hand, and said: Welcome, roommate! Great! he exclaimed. Let me grab my stuff from the car. Car? He clip-clopped on the hardwood floors to the front door, doing a little dance as he went, and I suddenly realized that his hooves hadn't made any noise that I can remember when I was showing him the apartment. Now they were loud and scratching up the floor. I wondered if I were screwed. Well, I was. Fucked up the ass by Satan himself. Not literally of course. But it hurt just the same.

I followed Satan to the door and watched as he clip-clopped down the brick walkway to the sidewalk. I looked to the left and then the right of my four-unit apartment building just in case any of the other tenants were watching from their doors, but no one was around. I turned back to Satan as he walked up to an ancient, cream-colored Ford Falcon with a big, faded *McCain/Palin* sticker that seemed to be the only thing keeping a battered chrome bumper attached to the car. That tiny Falcon was filled to the gills with all of his crap. There was even a futon rolled up in there. When he got the car door open, he turned and gave me this sad little boy look: Will you help? his eyes said. Sigh. I'm a sucker for sad eyes. I helped unload his shit. When it was all set up in his room, Satan turned to me, grinned, opened his arms wide, and said, Bring it in, brah! Brah? Fuck me. Fuck me. Fuck me. *Fuck. Me.* I brought it in and fell into Satan's musky embrace.

That first night, Satan made his allegedly famous spaghetti from things I already had in the kitchen. He also threw together a nice little cucumber and tomato salad, uncorked a bottle of Chianti. It was actually kind of nice, eating with someone instead of sitting in front of my laptop watching *30 Rock* reruns on Hulu and wolfing down some kind of crap sandwich. And Satan had some pretty funny stories. He could really set a scene, man. I give him that. He eventually told me how he ended up in his private pool of shit juice, to use his words. Seems he had been heavily invested in the stock market before the crash of '08. He also had a lousy adjustable rate thirty-year mortgage on his house in Encino. Well, you know the story, Satan said as he leaned back and took a sip of wine. A lot of poor folks ended up the way I did. Lost everything. The house, furniture . . . even my Mercedes-Benz S600 . . . oh, man, that was a sweet ride! Then he leaned forward, sticking his little goatee almost into what was left of my spaghetti. But I'm coming back, he whispered. People don't realize it because people are generally stupid, but the market is the place to be because you can only go up, right? The Dow will break fourteen thousand again, I promise you.

At this point in the conversation I got a little scared. I mean, he was talking crazy shit. He had that look in his eyes just like my dad when *he* came up with *his* insane schemes to make money. And where did it lead him? Broken-hearted, poor, and dead, that's where. But I listened to Satan spin his tales of future riches and actually hoped things would turn around for him.

Anyway, that was the last meal he cooked for me. From then on, it was roommate hell. Literally, I guess.

TRANSGRESSION #1: I have—or should I say, had—a top-of-the-line, old school Denon turntable that I paid dearly for in 2003 to play my pretty impressive collection of blues records. A collection that would make your head spin on its axis. Mississippi Fred McDowell. Lightin' Hopkins. Elmore James. Otis Rush. Robert Lowery. You know, *real* blues. Heartbreaking lyrics. Jammin' rhythm piano. Major key tonality. Sexy slide guitars. Raspy, mean-ass harmonicas. None of that commercial imitation claptrap. A collection that I'd been creating since I was in high school when my friends were listening to shit like the Foo Fighters, Oasis, and Collective Soul.

So one afternoon I get back from meeting with that solo practitioner to get a couple of research jobs and I hear "Everyday I Have the Blues" from one of my all-time favorite albums, *Otis Rush—Live at Montreux 1986.* Performing with Eric Clapton and the great Luther Allison doing vocals. Eddie Lusk on keyboard. I mean, what the hell? When I get into the apartment, I can't believe the scene: my albums are scattered all over floor, black vinyl everywhere. The Devil is on the couch humping this cheap-ass, meth-head skank who is moaning and screaming in beat with Rush's electric guitar licks. Empty Samuel Adams bottles everywhere. A bong the size of my forearm on the coffee table. The room stank of mota, sex, and beer mixed in with a whiff of ass. When the Devil realized I was standing there, he looked up, lost the gross grin, and mouthed: Oops!

TRANSGRESSION #2: He would steal my Honey Nut Cheerios,

one bowl at a time, every other day. But what really pissed me off was that he denied it when I confronted him. Honey Nut Cheerios? he asked. Me? I hate the stuff. Too sweet. I have to be careful because diabetes runs in my family. Me, I'm a Raisin Bran man myself.

TRANSGRESSION #3: The last straw, as they say, involved my mother. Okay, don't start cringing. It's nothing like that. The Devil did not molest my mother. Sadly, it was the other way around. Mom came by to drop off some mail that had ended up at her place for some odd reason even though I hadn't lived with her for so many years. But when she handed it to me, it was mostly junk mail. So I realized that she just wanted to see the roommate I had been complaining about for months. The Devil was sitting in my favorite (and only) recliner, reading the *Wall Street Journal*, one hairy goat leg crossed over the other, cup of French roast on the lamp table to his left. I have to admit, he was getting his shit together. Better groomed. Doing crunches each night so that his paunch had been replaced by a bit more definition in his abs. Even his horns were looking sharper. And of course, the moment Mom set eyes on him I knew what was going to be in her future. Ever since Dad died, Mom slept with anything that had a dick and at least one ball. I sighed, went into the kitchen to get her a Diet Coke. And when I came back, I saw them: Mom was on her knees sucking off the Devil, the Devil's eyes were closed, his head back, enjoying it. Then he opened his eyes and mouthed: Oops!

So, you see, my brain is now permanently scarred. It's been two months since the Devil finally left, three full fucking years as my roommate. He made a killing in the market . . . he was right about that Dow Jones. Bought a huge place in Malibu off of Pacific Coast Highway, right on the beach, not far from his cousin, La Diabla. But I finally got rehired by my old law firm so I don't need to sublet the extra room anymore. The economy is picking up. Obama won a second term. Monthly job reports looking steady if not on fire. Things are improving, no doubt. But I do believe that I will be haunted, forever, by that one bad decision.

My advice: never, never, never sublet to the Devil. You will live to regret it. I promise you. End of story.

Needle

Fátima's mother nudged her daughter and whispered: "Mija, go and say good-bye to your brother." Fátima's left eye twitched and she shifted in the pew. The hard wood made her tiny rump throb with soreness. She lifted her head, squinted, and focused on the gleaming, light blue twenty-gauge steel casket that stood before the altar.

Padre Espinoza had positioned himself to the right of casket, head bowed, eyes locked on his congregation, waiting for family members and friends to begin the solemn procession by the body. From his vantage point he could not see the body. He preferred it this way. The priest had done this so many times he eventually devised a game where he had to guess who would be the first to break down (someone always broke down), body shuddering with grief, shaking hand stroking the face of dearly departed. His track record was quite remarkable, about eighty percent correct over the course of a decade. Who would it be this time? Would it be Regina Quesada, the young man's widowed mother? No. She was strong. When her husband died three years ago, Regina was a rock. Not a tear. No gnashing of teeth. No rending of garments. Who would it be? Who would it be?

Fátima's mother nudged her daughter again, this time harder, so hard Fátima almost fell out of the pew. "He was your only brother," she hissed. "Say good-bye to him. Now."

Fátima had known this moment would come. She was prepared. She slowly lifted her little blue vinyl purse by the fake gold chain, stood, and took a deep breath. Her mother nodded at this moody cipher of a twelve-year-old daughter. This one who had worshipped her now dead older brother. How could she be so heartless?

Padre Espinoza lifted his head an inch, focused on Fátima, who stood near her sitting mother, and encouraged with an almost imperceptible smile this slight but beautiful girl to come forward and be the first to look upon the body. Would she be the one to break down? No, probably not. The priest shifted his eyes and scanned the congregation. A full house. The entire parish was here to say good-bye to one of their own. A war hero who served his country honorably in Afghanistan. But a foolish young man nonetheless, who slammed his Nissan Versa into an ancient oak in Topanga Canyon late one night after drinking too much. These poor boys and girls—and they were really just children—who come back from the horrors of war with little to prevent something like this. What a shame. What a waste.

Fátima now stood in front of the casket but kept her head up, eyes resting on the large crucifix behind the altar. She didn't need to see her brother's face. She'd seen it too many times, felt it close often enough, especially after he came back from the war. Fátima slowly unsnapped her purse and reached in.

The priest closed his eyes and sighed. He missed his own parents, both long dead. When they moved from El Paso to Los Angeles, he was two and they were barely out of their teens. They lived long enough to witness their only child take his final vows but not much more. The priest had been the one to break down first when his father died. His mother had to comfort her son, a grown man. But when his mother passed not more than a year later, the priest had to be strong because he was now truly alone.

Fátima's fingertips pressed gently within her small purse, feeling their way, in search of what she had placed within it early that morning. She kept her eyes on the crucifix, absorbed by Jesus' plaintive eyes looking upward to his father, asking for relief from suffering. Her fingertips recognized a crumpled Kleenex, three quarters, a Chapstick . . . and then . . . ah! That's it. Fátima's thumb and index finger closed upon what she had been searching for.

Why does God let bad things happen to good people? It was the question he hated most. Of course, he had answers to this ubiquitous query. Answers formulated by great theologians. *All have sinned and fall short of the glory of God; thus there is not a person who is purely good.* And: *There are no bad things, at least for those who love God.* Or: *So God can bring about a greater good.* He had offered these and other aphorisms to his congregants throughout the years. But Padre Espinoza had long ago lost faith in these answers. None of them made sense anymore. How could they?

Fátima lifted the long needle from her purse and looked down at it. She counted to three, leaned close to her brother, and pierced his cheek. Fátima was surprised at how easily it went in, a clear liquid oozing slowly from the point of entry. She felt brave, strong. She pulled it out and then put it in again, this time moving faster. Two times, and then three, four, five. Hitting bone. Over and over until her brother's cheek tore open. Six. Seven. Eight. Nine. And then she stopped. Nine. The number of times Fátima's brother put himself inside of her when their mother slept, late at night, down the hall. Nine times before that night he died. Twice before Afghanistan. Seven times after he came back two years later. Nine.

The priest's reverie broke when a woman gasped. Who was it? He looked at his congregants. It was the young man's mother, Mrs. Quesada, who now stood, mouth agape, hand pointing to the casket. The priest followed the woman's finger to Fátima, who stood by her brother's body, breathing heavily but smiling peacefully at the large crucifix as if she had seen a divine vision. The priest stared at this girl who looked so beautiful in the dim light of the church. Why was her mother upset? This is acceptance, thought the priest. This is what God desires from us. There is nothing wrong with this child of God. She is perfect in every way.

Orange Line

We sit on the bench waiting for the Orange Line. Rosario reads a Bolaño novel that I gave her last week for her twenty-fourth birthday. In truth, I'd bought it for myself, but I couldn't get past the first thirty pages so I wrapped it in some nice gold wrapping paper, bought a card with a smiling monkey on it (you can't go wrong with a monkey card), and gave it to Rosario. She loved it, wondered how I knew she wanted to read it. I shrugged. Brilliant, I guess.

I should have brought a book with me. Rosario is buried in Bolaño and I just look around. No one is here but us. And a long-haired throwback to the seventies who sits on the next bench over to my right. Rosario sits to my left. Where is everyone? It's Tuesday morning. Yes it's early, but don't people work anymore? Funny question since I don't work, not right now. Between jobs, as they say. And Rosario is getting her master's in English literature at CSUN, so she's not really working either.

I hear a clicking sound and turn. It's the hippie clicking with his tongue. But he stops now that he has my attention. He smiles. He's too young to be missing teeth, but he appears to have only about six or seven left in his mouth. He clicks again and I turn to Rosario to see if she notices. Nope. She's in love with Bolaño. She's even smiling. She's on page 123.

The hippie clicks again so I turn back to him. He isn't smiling anymore. In fact, he looks pissed. Not just I-spilled-my-coffee-on-my-new-pants pissed. But a really I-will-kill-you-you-son-of-a-bitch pissed. He leans on his left arm so that he can get closer to me without getting off his bench. He leans, squints, and whispers:

Mexican.

I blink. I look over at Rosario but she keeps on reading.

You're a Mexican, he says.

I turn back to the hippie. So it's a cool Tuesday morning, my girlfriend and I wait for the Orange Line to get to the Red Line so we can make my appointment downtown. And this hippie with no teeth is calling me a Mexican, which I am. Well, actually Chicano, but close enough. I just don't need a toothless hippie to tell me what I already know. And besides, the hippie could be Mexican también based on his looks. Or he could be Peruvian, or Columbian, or something else, but certainly Latino if not Mexican per se. As I ponder the reason for the hippie's concern for my ethnic heritage, he adds:

And a Jew, too.

He licks his lips after saying this. If it weren't for the missing teeth and unkempt hair, the hippie would be somewhat handsome. But this is beside the point. The point is, how does he know that I'm a Jew? I converted four years ago. A point of contention between me and my Roman Catholic girlfriend. But I'm ten years older than Rosario, been married once before. I've lived. I'm complicated. And I'm a Jew. The hippie couldn't know that. My religion, that is, not my complexity.

The hippie doesn't give up.

A Mexican Jew, he hisses.

I shift, not believing what he is saying.

Or is it a Jewish Mexican, he muses almost to himself, considering the options.

I turn to Rosario. She smiles, gently, lovingly, at Bolaño, of course.

Did you hear what he said? I ask her.

Rosario doesn't look up from her book. I nudge her. She blinks and comes out of her love trance.

What? she says.

Him, that guy, I say, jerking my head in the hippie's direction.

Rosario looks past me. Then she looks into my eyes and sighs.

No one's there, she says.

I turn toward the hippie. He smiles and licks his lips until they gleam like sardines.

I turn back to Rosario, who hasn't moved her eyes.

One Mississippi, two Mississippi, three Mississippi . . .

I know no one's there, I finally say, adding a little laugh to sound believable.

One Mississippi, two Mississippi . . .

Rosario laughs and looks relieved. She pats my arm and turns a little too quickly back to Bolaño.

I look over at the hippie who still sits on the other bench, staring at me. I now hate him. I turn to stare ahead of me, at the parking lot. Three large crows pick at a greasy Carl's Jr. bag. One crow, the largest of the three, hits a gold mine of fries and jumps back carrying two in its beak. The other two crows dive deeper into the bag, excited, in a fever now that breakfast has been uncovered. The hippie starts his clicking again. I keep my eyes on the crows. I will not look at the hippie. I will not look at the hippie. I will not look at the hippie.

I should have brought a book to read.

Carbon Beach

Hernán Tafolla stared into Detective Ana Urrea's eyes. At sixteen, Hernán stood as tall as the detective, whose light brown eyes reminded him of the hot chocolate milk he drank each morning before walking to school. Deep. Rich. Delectable. As he and the detective stood off to the side, five police officers milled about the beach, not too far from the man's head that poked out from a mound of sand a few yards from the constant tide. If Hernán squinted, the head looked as though it had been severed from its body. But no. Nothing so exotic. Just a dead body covered up to its chin in sand. As the detective asked questions, Hernán could hear the waves hitting the wet sand, sea gulls calling out to each other, and the Sunday traffic emanating from the Pacific Coast Highway up past the beautiful homes. He heard an officer say that David Geffen lived in the house directly behind the head. Hernán discovered it shortly after walking through the public access way from the sidewalk to the sand. He finally had a driver's permit and drove all the way to Malibu from the Valley to enjoy some solitude with an early morning stroll on the beach. The head had been covered by an inverted blue ice chest, like the one Hernán's uncle Rudy always brought to Shadow Ranch Park in Canoga Park for family fiestas. At least that's what Hernán told the police and then repeated it to Detective Urrea, who now questioned Hernán with greater depth as they waited for his mother to get there. She blinked, once and then again, and shielded her eyes—those beautiful eyes—from the bright August sun. Detective Urrea's lips moved slowly, and Hernán noticed that she had nearly perfect teeth, straight and white except for a bit of red lipstick that had smudged onto one of her upper front teeth. She wanted Hernán to try very hard to remember if he'd seen any suspicious persons nearby. Hernán furrowed his brow, went deep into his memory, trying to come up with something. He knew then that he loved the detective. No doubt. A perfect love for a perfect woman. Hernán had to win her over. He was already partway there with his remarkable discovery of the man's body. Who else would have bothered to look under the ice chest? Only a dynamic, mature-for-his-age, quick-thinking young man. Yes, Hernán will help in the investigation and Detective Urrea will have no choice but to return his love. And because Hernán knew a lot about the man's death—too much, if truth be told—he would have every opportunity to make Detective Ana Urrea his. All he needed to do was remain calm. What was that word his English teacher taught the last week of school? Insouciance. Yes, that's it. *In-sou-ci-ance.* He must demonstrate insouciance, a lack of concern, indifference. That way, no one would be suspicious. Hernán never failed to do something once he set his mind to it. And he wouldn't fail now.

Imprints

Yeah, I'll have another. Liz? Are you sure? Okay. Just one more for me. But this time no salt on the rim. Thanks!

Look at that tuchis! So? I don't care if he's a waiter. Can't I enjoy the scenery? God, Liz, you *are* a snob *and* so traditional, aren't you? We've just entered a new millennium, my friend. Anyway, where was I? Oh, yeah. Like I said, my routine Monday through Friday is pretty much set. I get up about six-thirty and feed my fish and get the *New York Times* from my doorstep and make coffee and try to wake up. It's been pretty empty ever since I kicked Tobias out. God, what a name. Tobias. Of course, with a name like that he had to be handsome, a great fuck, a poet, and a cheat. Like my Pop says, "No hay rosa sin espinas." You know, Liz: there's no rose without thorns. Didn't you take something like four years of Spanish at that silly little liberal arts college you went to, what was it? Anyway, my teeny-tiny apartment feels pretty big without Tobias knocking around it. What? Cats? No way. I don't have cats because I'm allergic and besides I don't want to be a cliché: professional single woman in her mid-thirties—okay, thirty-nine—living alone in New York. With a cat. I didn't have allergies until I left L.A. for Stanford. That was the year California was suffering from a horrible drought. So for some reason that made the hay fever season one of the worst in sixteen years or something like that. So my body suddenly says, "You're going to have allergies!" And ever since then I've been allergic to everything, especially cats. I don't really hate them, but they would be a lot easier to deal with if you could laminate them.

Oh, thank you. You're a doll . . . Jeremy. Give me the check. My treat, Liz.

Oh, this tastes good. What? Why shouldn't I call him by his name? That's why they wear nametags.

Anyway, when I went home for Christmas break that year, I couldn't even come close to our Siamese cat, Susie, because in about an hour I sounded like I had the flu. Mom wasn't so happy. She says, "Sandra, you've got to see a doctor." Pop, being the voice of reason, says, "¡Qué va!" which means "Nonsense!" Whenever Pop gets emotional, he reverts to Spanish.

They're quite a combination. Mom's second-generation Irish and Pop's Mexican, born and raised in a little town in the state of Jalisco called Ocotlán. They met when Pop came up to L.A. looking for work back in the fifties. He answered an ad for a little apartment on Pico Boulevard not too far from downtown and Mom was the manager. Pop says he fell in love fast and hard with that little redhead, and Mom says Pop was handsome and kind and spoke horrible English. The *I Love Lucy Show* was really big back then so they had a little running joke where Pop called Mom "Lucy" and Mom called Pop "Ricky." Of course, Pop isn't Cuban, but it almost matched perfectly. Yeah, I know. Too cute. But I should be so lucky.

Anyway, professionally, I've been using Mom's maiden name, O'Donnel, instead of Ramirez because I didn't want to be pigeonholed with any of the houses or their editors. I didn't want them to see me and think, "Oh, she must be pushing the next Cisneros, Villaseñor, or Anaya." If I have a good manuscript by a Latino or Latina writer, I want to push it without any baggage like that. Well, maybe I am being a little sensitive but I talk from a life of experience, girlfriend. Like when I got into Stanford and Mom took me to the Bullocks Wilshire to get a bunch of new clothes and the goddamn saleswoman says to Mom how nice it is that she's taking her *maid* out shopping! Just because I'm dark like Pop. But Mom keeps her cool and calmly says that I'm her daughter and that I got into Stanford and how I've been an A student all through Immaculate Heart High and all that. The saleswoman blushes six colors of red and that was that. I know that sounds stupid, but the publishing business is just like life in that way. It's not all that logical. Just look at the *New York Times* Bestsellers List. Does *the list* make sense? Case closed.

Are sure you don't want a sip? Okay. So, like I was saying, my routine is pretty much set. After getting ready, I take the subway and get in my office by about nine-thirty or ten and my three college students are already working away reading proposals and synopses and putting all those unsolicited manuscripts into one of three slush piles: HOPELESS, VERY HOPELESS, and FORGET ABOUT IT! If I only knew how this business worked when I was trying to get an agent for my first novel—my only novel—I doubt I'd have gone through the trouble. After sending it to about sixteen agents and receiving sixteen very polite form rejections, I decided to do a focused submission to a few small presses and got it published. It didn't do too badly. Well, it didn't do so great, either. So I'm a literary agent now.

Anyway, once I'm in and get another cup of coffee and grab a bagel from a huge pink box that one of my favorite students always brings in—Celeste is her name, I just love her—I start calling editors, leaving messages and looking into the status of some of my "hot properties"—I hate that term—and then it's time for lunch. After lunch I've got to get the submissions ready, so that requires getting the troops away from reading the mail to start Xeroxing and set up packages to get out to Federal Express by four to various editors. I'm out the door by five-thirty or six and back in the subway. I never read new proposals or manuscripts while at the office. That's for home—at night—and on the weekends. No, I'm not complaining. I'm trying to tell you about Robert. I'll get there.

Lunch. Pop doesn't understand why I call lunch the mother's milk of my business. "Mija, lunch is for relaxing. Otherwise, your stomach can't digest," he always says. "But not in my business," I always answer. "I make most of my deals at lunch." I know he'll never understand, or at least he'll always pretend not to understand. He works hard as a mechanic at, you know, the Rapid Transit District or the Metro or whatever they're calling it now. And he knows when he has to work and when he can relax and eat. Poor Pop. And I make three times his salary but I think I don't work as hard as he does. But he's proud of his only hija. It could have been worse, he knows, because my cousin Virna was one step away from being in a gang and her mom, my aunt Gloria, had to pick up and move out of L.A. to the San Fernando Valley. And it worked, thank God. Virna finished high school and has been waitressing at Jerry's Famous Deli for a few years now and is doing okay. But Pop is really proud of me.

So, lunch. Today I had lunch with Robert from an imprint of one of the major houses. My brother Dennis, the baby lawyer, hates that word *imprints* because, as he says in his deep lawyer voice, "They're 'subsidiaries.' Why would anyone call them 'imprints'? It sounds like you're pressing flowers or something." Dennis is so sincere about such things. What do you mean he's right? Oh, all you lawyers stick together. Where was I? Oh, yeah. Robert used to be with Random but left a couple years after that horrible purging— you know—when André Schiffrin left. I like André so much. A mensch!

Anyway, Robert left and there was a rumor that he was involved in André's leaving but I don't believe it. Robert has a lot of faults, but lack of loyalty is not one of them. But I'm torn about all this because Random gave two of my favorite writers *huge* deals and their books have been on the *New York Times* Bestsellers List—hey, sometimes the list makes sense—so I like André *and* Random. And those two writers are Hispanic, too.

God, these mini-quesadillas are great! You can have the last one. Are you sure? Okay. But I gotta get to the gym tomorrow morning. Anyway, I *hate* that word. *Hispanic*. It's so government-talk and sounds like antiseptic, white liberalese. No offense. My two Random stars are Chicano and Chicana. And Random signed them. ¡Bravo, Random! But I like André so much! My Catholic guilt is showing.

I'm getting there. Today was my lunch with Robert. Sometimes he reminds me of a character from Updike; you know, when Updike is taking his digs at the way publishing has become and comparing it with the old days. Robert's been in the business for almost thirty years, but he keeps up with the times and knows how to package a property and get his imprint on board. He always sees the movie or television angle of manuscripts. Truly goddamn amazing. Sometimes, though, he sounds so cynical dissecting a property and trying to figure the angle. That's when Updike is one hundred percent right on. But I like Robert.

So I got to the restaurant right on time, twelve-fifteen, but Robert was already there. The maître d', Alejandro, is this gorgeous Puerto Rican guy who looks great in a tux and just loves me. Says I look "muy triqueño"— you know, dark the way he thinks beautiful women should look.

"How's the novelist?" he says as I walk up to his little podium.

"Muy bien," I say.

He smiles and points over to Robert. "The old man is here already. Want me to walk you to your table?"

"No thanks," and I head to the table as I press a twenty into Alejandro's waiting hand. Why not? He's nice and he always squeezes me in. So? If he wants to get into my pants, so what?

Anyway, Robert sees me and stands up to give me a too tight hug. He says, "Sandra, that dress looks great on you."

I like compliments but Robert always goes just a little too far.

"It shows off your curves wonderfully! Been working out?"

See! So I ignore his leer and say, "What? This old schmatte?" Why do you laugh when I use Yiddish? Come on, Liz. Everyone does.

Where was I? Oh, yeah. Robert's on wife number two—no, wait, number three—and he can't help but flirt. He's not bad looking. Third- or fourth-generation German. Thin. Very thin. His hair is all gray now but he has lots of it and it looks great. He kind of reminds me of Gregory Peck but not as manly. He's shorter than you'd expect. With me standing five-foot-eight, and then add my heels, I tower over him. And he wears these beautiful suits. God! You just want to rub your hands all over the fabric so badly! Don't give me that look, Liz. I don't want to sleep with him. Jesus Christ, it's always sex with you.

Anyway, even though I start sitting, Robert says, "Sit, sit. I've already ordered for the both of us. The halibut. Your favorite."

Shit! I think. I hate it when he orders for me. I had halibut once and told him I liked it so now he thinks that I must have it every time we eat there. All I wanted was a little salad after my splurge last night. No comments, Liz. I'm allowed to splurge two nights in a row.

So Robert continues: "And I've ordered a small mixed for you, too."

Goddamn him! But I smile and say, "Robert, thank you. You're so thoughtful."

Okay. So, I'm a chickenshit. Anyway, we go through some old business and he's actually very well behaved. Eventually the salads come and we start to get to some new stuff.

"Robert, I have a wonderful new writer for you," I say.

"Oh?" he says.

"He's written a beautiful short novel."

"You mean a novella? You know nothing under fifty thousand words sells unless you're a big name already. Can it be expanded? How many words is it now?" God, of course I know how a novella is defined. But he likes to lecture. So, time to regroup. How do I bring him in?

"It's longer than *The Old Man and the Sea*. About as long as *Remembering Laughter*."

His jaw literally drops. He says, "Jesus Christ, Sandy, you're getting all Phi Beta Kappa on me. Hemingway? Stegner?"

So I back off and think fast: "Okay, okay. How about *The House on Mango Street*?"

"All right, that's a little better, but *Mango Street* was a total fluke and you know that. Besides, that was, what, fifteen years ago? My dear, say hello to Y2K . . . it's a lovely new millennium."

Yeah, well, I guess you're not the only one who needs reminding what year it is. Anyway, did I let his dis of my all-time favorite book stand unchallenged or did I move on? Maybe a salad fork shoved gently but firmly into his left eye would have been good. Sorry if that grosses you out, Liz, but that's what I thought.

So I say, "It was a great book. A watershed in ethnic literature that's on hundreds if not thousands of school reading lists across the country."

Robert gives me a look that says, "Don't lecture me about my business." But he controls the impulse because I've hit him where it matters: sales.

"How many words is this new *Mango Street*?"

"Thirty thousand plus."

"POV?" You know, Liz. Point of view. Right. You lawyers are worse with your legalese.

Anyway, I answer: "First person in the prologue and epilogue— through the eyes of the grandson reminiscing—and then third-person omniscient for the intervening chapters."

"Title?" he asks.

"*The Courtship of María Rivera Peña.*"

"Catchy. Sort of like *The Courtship of Eddy's Father.*" Robert closes his eyes as he says this. The restaurant grows hotter and noisier and I notice other agents sitting talking to other editors. And we're all trying to ignore each other's presence. What a goddamn business. Robert eventually wakes up from his trance: "Should be shorter, though. How about, *The Courtship of María Peña?*"

I say, "No, because the name Rivera has symbolism to it. Besides, that's not how Mexican names work."

"Symbolism?"

"Yes. *Rivera* means 'riverbank.'"

"Go on," says Robert as he puts more food into his mouth. For a thin man, he sure knows how to eat.

"And her husband-to-be is named Isla."

"So?"

"You know, 'riverbank' and 'island.'"

"Oooohhh. Good. Very good. Cute."

Robert always likes things like that. Good boy, Robert.

And then he ruins it: "I like that. And it kind of evokes Geraldo Rivera, too."

You like Geraldo, Liz? God, why are we friends?

Anyway, he says, "Okay. Ethnic writer?"

"Yes. Hispanic."

I know, I know. But Robert can't deal with terms like *Chicano*. Liz, when in Rome . . .

"Go on," Robert says. Then the waitress comes by with our lunch and someone else swipes my salad before I realize what's happening.

Anyway, I say, "Imagine a smaller *Joy Luck Club* or *Roots*."

Robert's face lights up like my computer screen. "There's that kicking fetus of a mind that I know and love."

Damn! That's a test! Who wrote 'kicking fetus of a mind'? I couldn't remember. Woolf? Hemingway? No, not Hem. Stein? Who was it? Oh, yeah!

"You shouldn't steal from Fitzgerald, especially from an unfinished manuscript."

I know I'm good, Liz.

"Now, that's my Stanford Phi Beta Kappa talking," he gushes.

Yup. Don't mess with my bad ass. Anyway, he's interested now.

"Movie potential," Robert continues. "Could Edward James Olmos play the lead? I like him. He was the soul of *Miami Vice*."

Maybe a fork in each eye would have been appropriate. What? You agree with him? That's not the point, Liz. Besides, you were too young to get into *Miami Vice*. Oh, never mind.

So I go along for the ride because he's interested and I say, "Yes, Olmos probably could play the lead when the protagonist is a little older. After he's married. And Los Lobos could do the soundtrack, you know, do some traditional Mexican music with their own modern twist just to mix it up some."

Then there's silence. Just the sound of Robert chewing on his duck intermingled with the din of the lunch crowd. He always orders duck. Then he startles me.

"Can't think about it. I'm on a self-imposed moratorium on ethnic writers." As he says this, he lifts his glass of ice tea to his lips but doesn't drink. He just holds it there, suspended like it was hemlock and he knew that it would be his last drink.

I didn't know what to say. A hot property was a hot property! Robert didn't care who wrote the book as long as it was good and could sell well.

"What do you mean?" was all I could manage to say. I felt deflated.

"I'm getting a reputation."

"What?" I sputter.

Then he starts: "I'm getting a reputation with some people-on-high as a promoter of ethnic writers, and that's not the rep I want. Too limiting. It also makes me look too liberal. Someone like Rush would never come to me. Remember what happened to André? That's why he was shown the door." I swear to God he said it. And he puts another piece of duck in his mouth. I tell you, I could've shat right there.

So I say, "So what? You're a success. Your books sell. What more do they want?"

Robert starts to smile. Slowly at first. Then a full-faced, goofy grin and then laughter. I think, what the hell's going on? Has he finally lost it completely?

"Gotcha!" he says as he lets out an uncharacteristic snort.

I think, that little son of a bitch!

And then I say, "Robert, you son of a bitch!"

He wipes a tear from his eye because he's been laughing so hard. "Sandy, you've got to lighten up a bit," he says. "You've brought me wonderful projects and almost a quarter of them are ethnic. They've done pretty well. And even though you're nothin' but a white girl, you're my best source for that kind of work."

What did I say? I said, "Half white." No shit. Guess I was just pissed.

"What?" he stammers.

"My father is Mexican. Born in Mexico. Mom's Irish." And I let out a big breath.

Robert freezes for about twenty seconds. At first he realizes that his little joke hit closer to home than he planned. Then I could see him searching his memory for any racist remark he might have said. Did he ever talk about "wetbacks"? I think he couldn't remember anything so he looks relieved. Then he searches my features to see if he could discern my hot Aztec blood. His face suddenly lights up.

"I should have known! I see it now! That's why you're so beautiful in that exotic way. Not quite white, not quite ethnic."

Oh, God, I think. Not this shit. Hey, Liz, you don't get this stuff. It gets old, fast.

Robert then says, "Why do you go by O'Donnel?"

And I explain. And the more I explain, the madder he gets. Finally, he says, "Sandy—if that's really your name . . ."

Ouch! He knows how to throw 'em.

"Sandy, do you know how many Hispanic agents there are in New York? Huh? Do you? You could be one of a handful, and you go by O'Donnel! That's plain stupid! By the way, what is your father's name?"

I say, "Ramirez."

"Beautiful!" he almost yells.

Then there's silence, which is very unusual for Robert and me.

"Look," he begins slowly. "I'll read that novella. I feel exhausted. It's very strange to know someone for eight years and find out she's really someone different."

Robert can be so dramatic sometimes. But I like that about him. Anyway, as we finish our lunch we talk about our lives instead of projects. Though he's a flirt, he suddenly becomes more relaxed, more serious. No, Liz, it wasn't just an act. He got *real*. So I learned that his daughter from his first marriage was just finishing at Brown and was interning for one of the houses. His son was doing great in high school. Very athletic. Football, for Christ's sake! His current wife, Marilyn, started writing short stories and one of them was just accepted by *Glimmer Train Stories*. It's one of those literary journals that are piled all over my apartment. Anyway, Robert looks so full of pride as he tells me how it was her very first submission. And—I couldn't believe it!—Robert has a seventy-five-thousand-word novel on his hard drive at home but he's never submitted it to anyone! It's loosely based on *his* great-grandparents' trek to the United States from Germany and their settling in the Midwest. So I encourage him to submit it to André, and he laughs and says that I shouldn't think that he hasn't thought of it. When we finish our lunch, he looks at me with eyes more like my father's than that of a fifty-five-year-old sex maniac. Really.

So, we eventually get up to go and Alejandro gives me a little wink as Robert and I walk out. Robert flags a taxi for me even though I'm quite capable of doing it myself, but he's just that way. We hug, without a word, I hop in, and Robert closes the door with a quick flick of his wrist. And I head back to my office to make my West Coast calls before those folks go to their lunches. But first I talk to my secretary. I'm getting there, Liz. I know it's late.

Anyway, I say, "Ray, could you order some new cards and stationery?"

Ray looks up from his daily Swiss on rye with lettuce and lots and lots of tomatoes. He always has little treats waiting by his sandwich. Today he's lined up six miniature Mounds bars to the right of the telephone looking like little parked cars. A can of Sprite stands watch over it all. He gives me a mournful look that's hard to take seriously, especially with his shaved head and very chic goatee. When he interviewed with me two years ago, he had nicely trimmed blond hair with a part on the side and absolutely no facial hair.

He says, "Why, Sandy? I just ordered them."

"I want my name to be changed." No shit, Liz.

And he looks bewildered. "To what?" As he says this, Ray puts his sandwich down for emphasis.

"To 'Sandra O'Donnel Ramirez.'"

Suddenly, Ray perks up. "You're getting married?"

I know. I laughed, too. But you know Ray. Always hopeful. Always old fashioned.

So I say, "No. I'll explain later." Then I reach down to Ray's desk and pick up some manuscripts that had been delivered during lunch while slyly swiping one of his Mounds bars and head to my office to start making my West Coast calls. Okay, that's what happened today. All right, all right. It's not such a big deal to you, but to me it is. Hold on. Let me put a nice tip here for, what's his name? Jeremy? Hey, it's my money. Besides, *Jeremy* did a *great* job. Okay. Let's go, Liz. I've gotta get up early to get to the gym. Hey, you know who just joined? I saw him last week on the StairMaster. You know, the guy from what's that show? The one you like. Yeah. That's him. No shit. But he looks better on TV.

Fat Man

You were once a fat man . . . but no longer. You lie on your lean, taut back, bed rumpled and musky, as she brushes her teeth, tiny Braun motor humming efficiently in the white-tiled bathroom. Your long fingers—no longer plump sausages—slowly massage a newly flat abdomen (Al Green flat, like his *Greatest Hits* cover), sliding down to the bony horns of your protruding pelvis, and finally reaching your flaccid, sated cock, which lies to one side (to the right, actually) content in the knowledge that it can spring to life, up and hard, without fear of bumping into, and fighting for air-space with, a selfish, globular belly. Your eyes ease open and you watch your hands on your cock (you can actually *see* it!) and your lids slowly close again and a smile appears on your lips. Now she can slide you into her, from on high or below, without a barrier, a wall (the wall came tumbling down!) preventing easy access. Ah! From above! She can now lie beneath you without fear of pain, fear of becoming a waffle. She can wrap her legs around her lean man and take him in, slide him in, guide him in, with ease. The Braun toothbrush clicks off and you hear her rinse and spit. And she emits a little laugh, an almost gleeful chortle as she saunters from the bathroom back toward the bed. Your eyes pop open in anticipation and see her beautiful, round body—pink with fat—soft like a down-filled, oversized pillow that you can disappear in. She loves you. And she wants you. Because you were once a fat man . . . but no longer.

Kind of Blue

1.

"So what?" says René. He adds a shrug for emphasis.

Silence. René just stares at me. And then another "So what?" It's not really a question. It's a statement. A declaration. A dare.

René wipes his nose on his torn shirtsleeve. He gets most of the blood and snot off his upper lip that had been seeping slowly from his nostrils. René holds his arm in front of him and examines the sleeve. His dark skin peeks out from the torn blue cotton. He blinks and then lets out a muffled laugh, as if he has just discovered five bucks in his pocket.

I can't stand seeing René's eyes when he gets like this so I turn and look over toward his apartment's kitchen window, which now has most of its glass piled up in jagged shards inside the sink and a few pieces on the floor. Big Man lays right there, on some of the broken glass. He's in a heap, like he's drunk or something. But he's not.

"So what?" René says again.

He follows my eyes over to Big Man.

"Fuck that pendejo," says René. "He tried to kill me, that fucker. You saw."

"But . . ." I start to answer.

"But the fuck what?"

I look down at my feet, tired of looking at Big Man, who really isn't very big. Maybe five-five, if that. Muy flaco, también. Skin and bones.

"Never mind," I say. "Forget about it."

"Damn straight," says René, victorious. "Damn straight."

2.

René gave us all names. His own little group, his followers. Branded us like cows with stupid little names.

René named Humberto "Big Man." Funny because he's so small. René made himself laugh with that one.

Big Man's little sister Sylvia is "Slinky" because she's kind of sexy in a weird way. Goth. Pierced left eyebrow, left nostril, and left cheek. She gives René blow jobs but they don't fuck. René says he has too much respect for Sylvia to stick her. Even though he doesn't—or didn't—think much of her brother. Sylvia turned fifteen last week. Big Man and me and René finish high school this year. Well, at least I will.

Anyway, René named me "Freddie Freeloader," which I hate. Kind of a fucked-up name, you know? It's just because of that time I bummed some mota off of René behind the dumpster at our high school. It was this one hot day during our Ancient Cultures class, which we cut at least twice a week. Just that one time I didn't have any weed on me. But then, right there, after passing over the joint real nice, he calls me Freddie Freeloader through tight lips, trying to keep the smoke in his lungs, but then he starts to laugh and then he chokes, tears running down his face, totally cracking himself up. After he calms down, René looks up at me and says, "You're Freddie Freeloader, Alfredo." He adds: "From now on."

And it's stuck with me for almost four years. René isn't called anything but his own baptism name. Nobody dares call him something else. Not me. Not nobody.

3.

Blue in green. Or is it green in blue? Anyway, that's Sylvia's eyes. They kind of glow with the two colors mixed in. Because her skin is real dark and her long hair shines black, Sylvia's eyes are the first thing you notice about her. They make her beautiful. At least, that's what I think. But whenever I start daydreaming about those eyes, that skin … my mind wanders to what I know she does to René and I feel sick. I don't understand it. It's fucked up. And it's going to get more fucked up when Sylvia finds out her brother's dead.

4.

"All Blues." That's the name I'd give René if I could. He'd probably kick my ass if I tried so I never even *thought* about saying it to his face. He always wears this long-sleeved blue shirt tucked into blue Dickies, the real loose kind. René even likes to put on these blue Chuck Taylors. Maybe he'd laugh, take it in stride, not care if I called him All Blues. But I doubt it. I mean, I try to act tough, but I'm nothing like René. Look at Humberto. Dead. In two seconds, before Humberto could even open the window and sneak in, René hears something, jumps up from the couch where we had been smoking and watching some stupid shit on TV in the other room, and runs into the kitchen before I know what's happening. That's the funny thing about René: he can be all fucked up on mota but he never gets fuzzy or out of control. He stays alert, like a fox. Or a snake. Or a rat.

Anyway, before I even realize he's run out of the room, I hear a grunt and then all this glass breaking. I freak out at this point and get to the kitchen as fast as I can, tripping over my untied shoes. And there I see Humberto on the floor, not moving, with broken glass all over the place. René is hovering over the body, his shirtsleeve torn and bloody, looking up at me and smiling.

5.

"Flamenco Sketches," whispers Sylvia. "That's what I call them."

She hands me one drawing, and then another. I don't know why Sylvia calls her pictures Flamenco Sketches. I don't see any Spanish dancers. Just black circles, going 'round and 'round and 'round from the outside edges to the center. But I don't criticize her. I just look at each one and nod like I really like the drawings. I don't know why she brought them here, of all places, but she has a right to do what she wants. Especially right now.

The church is crowded, people are crying, the priest is saying something over Humberto's coffin, which is closed. His mom's a mess, collapsed down into herself, weeping but not making a sound except for a moan that scares me. Sylvia finally puts the drawings down on the pew, leans her head into my shoulder, closes her eyes. I was surprised she wanted me to sit next to her with the family, but René was nowhere to be found so I guess she needs me. They don't blame him, not really, because I told everyone it was an accident. I had to.

I look around, see all of these people I've known since I was little. And then I see him, René, off at the side of the church, by the statue of Saint Thomas. You know, doubting Thomas, the one who didn't believe Jesus had come back from the dead. René turns his head just enough to stare back at me. And then he does it. He smiles. Just a little. With *that* look in his eyes. The same look I saw the night Humberto died. And I swear René starts to laugh, real quiet, but it's still a laugh. I turn away, feeling like I can't breathe, and then kiss the top of Sylvia's head. Her hair is so soft and smells good. "It's okay," I whisper. "It's okay."

La Diabla at the Farm

Ah, mis amigos. I have missed you so much! But you see, I needed some downtime, as my gabacho friends say. I needed to "recharge" myself. Partake in a little sopa de pollo para el alma. But I have returned, refreshed. My ch'i is back in balance, I have corrected the bad feng shui in my life, and I thank the powers-that-be that my house was not built facing a fork in the road, a dead end, or a valley. In short, all is well and I am ready to tell cuentos again.

¿Cómo? You think I joke? Oh, I would never joke of such things. Everyone must be in balance or else one cannot function as fully as one must. As my papá was fond of saying: El campo fértil no descansado, se tornará estéril. You know: The fertile field that is not given rest will become barren. Well, I was under great threat of becoming barren—spiritually speaking, of course. This is true of all living things. Even for the Devil. Yes, El Diablo. Or, as I've told you many, many times before, if you're in certain neighborhoods in Los Angeles, it's La Diabla. Because the Devil is legion; the Devil resides in most towns and cities and may be a man or a woman or both. It all depends on what is needed. So, apropos of my cuento for today, in some of the upscale areas of my beloved City of Angels, the Devil is very much female.

Well, one day back at the end of the seventies, when disco was still king and just before the Reagan years, things weren't going so well for La Diabla. Yes, she resided in a beautiful beachfront home at Malibu, which should make any soul feel refreshed each day. But remember that she had gone through all that loco shit with Don de la Cruz not to mention that crazy Quetzalcoatl. ¡Ay Dios mío! That was some crazy-ass crap, wasn't it? My cabeza starts to swim just thinking about it all! And though she's a bit modest, if push came to shove, La Diabla would admit to having something to do with some of the best evil that befell the world in the late seventies: Jim Jones and his little escapade in Guyana, the oil spill from the *Amoco Cadiz* off Brittany's coast, the rise of the Ayatollah Ruhollah Khomeini and Donald Trump, and the untimely death of Elvis. Legion always tapped her for the big jobs, even if it took her out of Los Angeles. Anyway, brilliant work if you think about it.

But spawning evil day in and day out can knock the stuffing out of anyone. ¿No? La Diabla couldn't get away from her work even living in beautiful Malibu. I mean, think about it: her neighbors were film and music people who could give her a run for her money when it came to committing depraved and degenerate acts. It all made her feel so weary. Even her boy toy, Eduardo, an "actor" who made his real living as a very fine waiter at the Good Earth restaurant in Westwood, began to bore her. Besides, he slept with her not because she was beautiful. Oh, no. As you know, any man who fucks La Diabla suffers horrible pain. Eduardo did the dirty deed because La Diabla had promised him great and future success as an actor. Anyway, La Diabla needed to get away for a while and recreate in the truest sense of the term. But where to go? What to do?

La Diabla had already traveled throughout the world, from Paris, Texas, to Paris, France. She had enjoyed all climates, innumerable foreign delicacies, every conceivable carnal delight. But those were working vacations, really. She toiled wherever she went, never resting even while taking great joy in spreading her spleen. One day, after feeling particularly fed up with it all, La Diabla sat in her study, closed her eyes, and let the rhythmic crash of the waves work on her subconscious. Where could she go? What would be different? New? Relaxing and refreshing? And then it came to her, in a burst, just like that. Palo Alto! She had of course been to San Francisco and Oakland and even Sunnyvale, but La Diabla had missed Palo Alto despite a very fine recommendation from one of her favorite disciples. This gentleman (let's call him "Simón") attended one of Stanford University's graduate programs (I won't divulge which one for obvious reasons) and in his spare time was a staff artist for Stanford's admirable and well-established humor magazine, the *Chaparral*. Simón's particular talent was embedding subliminal messages in his illustrations. These messages were not innocent ones to encourage the student body to drink Coke or buy Nike shoes. Oh, no. *His* subliminal messages encouraged Stanford's young folk to cheat on tests, haze neophyte fraternity brothers, listen to Boz Scaggs records, and buy additional copies of the *Chaparral* for loved ones.

In any event, Simón had always waxed eloquent when it came to life on "the Farm," as this fine university is called by all who love it. And he had nothing but praise for the surrounding communities of Palo Alto, Mountain View, Menlo Park, et cetera. All-meat pizzas at Fargos, sirloin steak burgers from Kirk's, TOGO's six-foot-long submarine sandwiches, a cool mug of beer at the Oasis. As you can see, Simón's life on the Farm revolved around food and drink. But he also sang the praises of the incomparable LSJUMB (those crazy pendejos make the football games so loco!), evening strolls along the Quad, visits to Hoover's last erection (Hoover Tower to you), and chatting about current events over a frothy latté at the campus coffee shop. It all seemed so relaxing to La Diabla. Why not stay near the Farm?

So La Diabla contacted a broker and located a wonderful house for lease on Cowper. Perfect setting: not too far from campus, nestled among other fine homes in Palo Alto with trees lining every street. And a bargain, too, though she really didn't need to worry about money. Who could ask for more? With a phone call it was all set. La Diabla would finally have a vacation, come back refreshed, and be ready to do battle with good once more. ¡Híjole! She was going to come back swinging like a drunken puta! She leased her Malibu abode to a record executive who had been kicked out of his Pacific Palisades mansion by his third wife, packed up a few things, and flew up north.

Settling into the quaint Palo Alto home took little effort. It fit La Diabla like the knitted leg warmers she was fond of wearing during the cool beach winters. The hardwood floors gleamed with new polish, and the Shaker furniture proved to be functional, comfortable, and oddly calming. Ah! The only thing that gave La Diabla the willies was Saint Anne's Church no more than three blocks away down her street. But she decided not to let the competition bother her. Two full months of no work, just relaxation. Right? Of course, right!

So time passed. One week, then two, now three. And with each day of doing nothing but strolling the finely manicured neighborhood with a few jaunts onto campus, La Diabla grew more and more relaxed. The worry lines on her beautiful brow began to recede, her frown softened sometimes into a small smile, her neck and shoulders loosened. Why hadn't she done this before? She knew the answer: La Diabla was a classic type A. No doubt about it.

Well, I wouldn't be telling you this cuento, mis amigos, if La Diabla's little vacation went swimmingly. No, that wouldn't be a story at all. So let's get down to it. ¿No? So I ask you: what would ruin such a perfect and well-deserved sabbatical from evildoing? Think hard. Remember my other tales of La Diabla? ¡Ándale! Got it? ¡Sí! Sex! La Diabla was missing *it* so bad! You know, she loved to have *it* in her all the time. Call *it* what you will: hueso, pistola, pinga, picha, bastón, camote, elote, bastardo, pito, chorizo, lechero, pirinola. Or, as you simple English speakers would say, dick. Nothing made her happier than to have one pulsating and thrusting in her nido, concha, tamal, pepa, mondongo, mamey, paloma, et cetera, et cetera, et cetera. She even daydreamed of her insipid young man back in Malibu. La Diabla needed a fuck right away. But all she seemed to appreciate were these Stanford undergraduates. Should she mess with such youthful specimens of budding manhood? It would be wrong, wouldn't it? Ah! So it would. Which is precisely why it would be so right for La Diabla. She is so evil and horny! A powerful combination. So, one morning as La Diabla tossed about in her lonely, clean sheets, she reached up and grabbed her own chichis and swore that she would get laid that very night! Oh, the horror of it all! I'm so relieved that my son went to Berkeley!

Because La Diabla hadn't gone to college she didn't realize how easy it would be for a woman of her beauty to land an undergraduate male, especially one attending the Farm. She could have her pick, as they say, particularly if La Diabla attended a fraternity rush party. But she was ignorant of such things. She needed help in figuring how to proceed. This could not end in failure for she would surely explode! La Diabla called her friend Simón, who luckily had not yet left his apartment for class.

"Simón," she purred into the receiver. "I need your assistance."

"Yes, mi amor," he purred back. "Anything. Except, you know."

And she knew what "you know" meant. Sex. You see, several years ago, after having a bit too much vino, Simón—who is a mortal—and La Diabla went for it. And as you might remember, when a mortal has sex with the devil, it ain't pretty. Oh, the pain! It is indescribable. So I won't even try. Even the booze couldn't numb poor, unsuspecting Simón. Thus, despite La Diabla's extraordinary pulchritude, Simón didn't want to hit *that* again. And La Diabla understood completely.

"Well, Simón," she continued. "I do need to have sex but I won't burden you with the deed."

Relieved, he said: "Ah, but you want me to set you up, right?"

"Any sexy friends?" she ventured as she let her left hand slide between her legs.

"Friends?" he said. "You don't need any of my friends. There are dozens of young men on campus who would kill to get some off you."

La Diabla loved the flattery. "So, how do I meet one?" Her fingers explored the wet folds of her womanhood.

"Meet me at the coffee shop at seven tonight."

"Really?"

"Really."

"Oh, yes!" she said as she climaxed.

Simón shook his head. "I won't disappoint you."

La Diabla couldn't answer. She dropped the receiver in its cradle with a *clack* and closed her eyes to dream away the morning in delicious anticipation.

She awoke at noon and spent her dear time bathing, dressing, and putting on makeup (or war paint as she liked to joke). La Diabla felt like a young girl again. It was all so exciting! What wonderful man would she have tonight? Who would suffer the exquisite torture of sex with La Diabla? The mystery made her dizzy with anticipation. To burn off some nervous energy, she put on Michael Jackson's *Off the Wall* album and danced around the house holding the album cover out in front of her like a partner. Oh, Mr. Jackson looked so handsome to La Diabla. Maybe she could find a man like him tonight! (Please do not be shocked . . . this was many years ago, remember?) She worked up such a sweat shaking her booty that she had to shower again. But no matter. All would be wonderful soon. Simón virtually guaranteed it!

La Diabla got to the Stanford coffee shop a bit early, giddy as a young girl, and ordered a glass of Chablis. She found an empty booth and perused the bustling room. Such good-looking young men everywhere! ¡Ay! Who would be in her tonight?

"Hey, chica, stop drooling," said a familiar voice.

La Diabla looked up and rested her eyes on Simón's tanned, angular face. She laughed.

"Oh, Simón, we could skip this hunt and go back to my house," she purred.

Simón held up a finger: "Un momento. Let me grab a beer."

When he came back, he took a long drink of his Anchor Steam and let out a tiny burp.

"You're so sexy when you're rude," whispered La Diabla as she reached for his knee, which made Simón jump.

"Mi cielo," said Simón as he stopped La Diabla's migrating hand, "let us stick with our plan."

"Si, mi amor," she said feeling a bit chastened. "Who do you have for me?"

Simón nodded backward. "Over there, by the painting of the old man."

La Diabla lifted her exquisite chin and narrowed her fiery eyes. In the corner sat a young man with dark, curly hair, a mustache, and a muscular build. Before him sat a coffee mug and a large textbook which he brushed back and forth with a yellow highlighter.

"Ah!" said La Diabla. "Muscles and brains. Not bad, mi amor, not bad at all."

Simón acknowledged the compliment with a self-satisfied grin.

"But how do I approach a college student?" she asked. "This is new to me, mi amor."

Simón leaned forward and whispered conspiratorially: "Easy. Take your wineglass and ask if he minds company."

La Diabla frowned. "Don't play with me. I'm so horny I could behead someone right now."

Simón knew she wasn't exaggerating because he once saw La Diabla kill for less. So he patted her hand and said, "I'm not joking. And then to break the ice, ask him what he's studying."

"Oh?"

"I guarantee you will be fucking him within the hour."

"Really?"

"Yes."

La Diabla asked: "Do you know him?"

Simón laughed. "No, not really. Not well. His name is Andy. Met him once at a party in Flo Mo. He's a junior, pre-med, and currently single. Broke up three weeks ago with a cute little sophomore from Casa Zapata."

Oh, mis amigos, such words made La Diabla squirm with sexual energy! A future doctor with the body and face of an actor who probably hadn't enjoyed any sex for a few weeks. How could she lose? Not possible. She squeezed Simón's knee in thanks, grabbed her wineglass, and made her way to Andy's table. After a few moments, he realized someone was standing over him. Andy looked up, a bit annoyed, but then his eyes widened as he took in La Diabla's beauty.

"Mind a little company?" she asked as her heart beat so hard it seemed to be traveling up her chest into her throat.

Andy offered a crooked smile. La Diabla loved crooked smiles. He stood, gave a slight bow, and pulled a chair out for her. She sat and crossed her long, smooth, brown legs.

"And who might you be?" he asked as he took his seat again.

Now this was a tough one. La Diabla had enjoyed many aliases throughout her centuries-long life. But she wanted something special for tonight. Something cheap, dirty, fuckable. Who should she be? She glanced around the room searching for an idea. Just then, a young woman walked by carrying several books including *Nicholas Nickleby*.

"Nicki," said La Diabla turning back to Andy. "With two *i*'s."

"Nicki with two *i*'s, I am Andrew," he smiled, "but call me Andy."

They sat in silence for a few moments basking in each other's admiration. Simón observed them from across the room feeling quite proud of himself.

La Diabla was ready to make her move: "So, what's your major?"

Andy grinned. "Hum Bio. I'm pre-med."

La Diabla had no idea what Hum Bio was but she certainly knew the meaning of pre-med. This pretty boy had brains.

"Well, you know what they say," she purred.

"What?"

"All study and no fucking makes Andy a boring boy."

Can you believe it, mis amigos? Such audacity! No woman has ever said such a thing to me and I'm not chopped liver! I've had a few chicas in my day. But this is loco! And what do you think Andy did? Well, he fell back in his chair, shook his head, and tried to respond. But not a sound came from his lips. La Diabla knew she had hooked him. So she played a bit with this poor boy.

"How about it?" she said and slid her foot up Andy's poor, unsuspecting right leg. He quivered at her touch.

Andy sputtered: "But I have a roommate."

La Diabla whispered: "I have a house in Palo Alto all to myself."

Oh, magic words indeed! Better than "I have a single in Serra." Andy became woozy with anticipation and the possibilities!

"Let's go!" he yelped like an excited puppy. And then he whispered: "I assume you have a car."

Of course La Diabla had wheels! And only the best: a cream-colored 1978 (then only a year old!) Mercedes convertible 450 SL with tobacco interior. A joy to ride with the top down on your way to get laid! ¡Chingao!

So they sped to La Diabla's rented house on Cowper, and, and, and . . . well, this is where my little cuento gets a bit strange. I'm not quite certain if this old hombre has the palabras to express precisely what happened next. Let me take a swig of my cerveza. Ah! That's better. Now a copita of Presidente. A reverse chaser! Okay, my lengua is loose, my mind is agile, and I think the words will now come.

This is what happened: they screwed in the hallway, they did it in the closet, they humped up the staircase, and did the fandango in all three bedrooms! For hours and hours they did not stop! La Diabla couldn't believe her luck to have hooked up with such a campus stud! And after a full twenty-four hours of this craziness, she had to rest, take a nap, to get ready for the next round. This is where it gets strange, mis amigos. La Diabla fell into the deepest sleep of her existence, and she dreamed! You see, she hardly ever slept and she certainly never dreamed. In her dream she strolled alone on the Stanford campus, peering into empty classrooms, gazing down deserted paths, listening to the complete silence of an abandoned university. This brought a chill to La Diabla's spine, something that was as alien to her as righteousness and piety. And in her dream she felt the anguish of solitude as complete and total as can be. So horrible was this feeling that a tear appeared at the corner of La Diabla's left eye and made its way, slowly at first, down her cheek and then sped off her face and splashed to the ground.

Then she woke! At first she forgot where she was. Then La Diabla heard Andy moving around in the bathroom. Oh, this Andy. What was he doing to her? He was different from the rest. He didn't feel the horrific pain when he put his manhood into La Diabla. Why not? What was different about him? But after a moment, it came to her. Andy merely lusted after La Diabla—for the beautiful woman she appeared to be—and he didn't know that she was the Princess of Evil. In other words, mis amigos, Andy didn't try to please La Diabla to get something in return such as great wealth or tremendous fame. No. His was an honest, heartfelt desire to fuck La Diabla.

And as the nickel dropped (to coin a phrase, pun intended), Andy opened the bathroom door, grinned a lascivious grin at La Diabla, and bounded back into bed. As La Diabla let this young man enter again, she shed another tear. For you see, she was falling in love. And we all know that La Diabla cannot allow herself to do such a thing. It would ruin her without a doubt, creating that one, true weakness in her being that would make her almost human. So, once they finished, she knew what she had to do to this mortal. There was no choice.

As Andy came for what would be his last time, he said, "Nicki, I love you."

"Yes, mi cielo," La Diabla whispered. "Te amo mucho."

Oh, such sadness, such romance . . . like a Juan Gabriel song. I'm getting a bit choked up just thinking of that poor lad, now long dead. I'm not quite certain that I have a moral for this little story. But I'm reminded of a dicho my abuelito was fond of: "El amor es el último que resiste morir." You know: Love is the last thing that dies. Perhaps it is. Perhaps it isn't. Ni modo. But for one poor Stanford pendejo—who should have known that this woman's offer was too good to be true—it doesn't much matter.

Mis amigos, that is the end of my cuento. There you have it. Sex. Death. Stanford. What more is there? Nada más.

Things We Do Not Talk About

Alma López stole six marbles from Joshua Braun, the boy who lived across the street and who secretly loved Alma. This is how it happened: Joshua had to pee, so he stood and ran to the bathroom. Alma was now all alone sitting at the rug's edge in Joshua's den staring at the large Tupperware container in front of her. She guessed that it held hundreds or even thousands of marbles. The late afternoon sun shone through the French doors, making the marbles' reds, greens, yellows, purples, and oranges glisten like hard candy. Alma listened to Joshua pee. She squinted and scanned the room even though she knew no one else was nearby. Alma closed her eyes, reached into the container, and grabbed six marbles. She didn't want to choose: Alma craved the randomness of the process. She shoved the marbles into her jeans pocket just as Joshua flushed. Alma opened her eyes and offered Joshua a broad smile as he trotted back into the den. Before Joshua could settle back onto the rug, Alma stood and said she needed to get home because it was almost dinnertime and her father would be angry if she didn't help set the table. In truth, her house was empty and she would have to heat up leftover chicken posole that her father had picked up from Grand Central Market the day before. Alma's father never got home before eight o'clock because of a lousy commute from downtown to Canoga Park. She liked her lie. It was perfect.

The six marbles would follow Alma all her life, even as she traveled to Cornell where she majored in English literature, back to California for graduate school at UCLA, and finally to the small but conveniently located Santa Monica apartment where she settled once she landed a job at the city college on Pico Boulevard where she taught Literature of the Bible and Images of Women in Contemporary Poetry.

Alma wondered what had happened to Joshua and whether he ever knew about the stolen marbles. He must have. Joshua kept track of everything because he was more intelligent than anyone she knew at that time. But they'd lost contact after Joshua's family moved to Phoenix at the end of sixth grade. He wrote three letters to Alma but she never wrote back. Joshua finally gave up, heartbroken. Alma's father found the first discarded letter in the kitchen trashcan, retrieved it, and put it on her little white desk. She threw it away, this time in the large trash bin at the side of the house. The other two letters met the same fate, each safely tucked under other rubbish so her father would not discover and salvage them.

Alma kept the six marbles on a bed of blue velvet in a small wooden box she bought in Mexico City one summer vacation with her father. She chose the box—a large, grinning skull carved onto its top—despite her father's attempt to steer Alma to something a little less morbid. But no, Alma wanted that box. Period. She loved skulls, if *love* is the right word. Alma remembered the trip as uneventful, even a bit boring. She had wished that her mother could be with her and her father. By this time Alma could barely remember what her mother's voice sounded like. Alma's father kept pictures of his late wife throughout the house so that Alma would remember her face. But it was her mother's voice she missed most.

After teaching for four years, and after her father passed away leaving her some money, Alma decided to buy a small house not too far from her college. It was time. Alma's father would have been proud of her making this very grown-up decision, no need for a man to make her life complete.

When the movers came, Alma had already packed everything. It wouldn't take long, especially because the company had sent two very large and efficient young men. They looked like her students—tattoos, ear gages, all-knowing smirks—except with more muscle. The move went smoothly. Alma tipped them generously and offered them cold bottles of water, a generosity her father had taught her through example.

Alma unpacked slowly, no need to rush, because she had the entire weekend ahead of her. She opened the first box, the one holding her old den's knickknacks. Alma found the box that held the six marbles. She opened it, half expecting them to be gone, perhaps stolen by one of the movers when she stepped away to the bathroom for a minute. That would be ironic, wouldn't it? But the marbles sat in the blue velvet, safe as ever. Alma closed the box and put it on the mantle of her rustic brick fireplace. There the box would sit, unopened, and moved only when Alma dusted.

Alma eventually became a full professor in the English Department, popular with her colleagues and students alike. One evening, after hosting a visiting novelist on campus, she came home to find the front door ajar. Alma immediately regretted not getting a home alarm system. Her father would have been disappointed. She walked over to the house of her neighbor, Scott, who would be having dinner with his partner, Jorge. Alma did not like Jorge. She thought him stupid. But she appreciated Scott for his love of literature and art. For this Alma felt guilty because Jorge was from modest means and Scott was "born on third base," as he readily admitted. But that is life, isn't it? Sometimes you like those born on third base more than those who have struggled. Nothing to feel guilty about.

Scott escorted Alma to her house, saying that it was probably fine; perhaps she'd forgotten to lock her door, that's all. Scott always stayed calm. Jorge stayed behind to continue eating dinner, never offering to come along. This reinforced Alma's negative view of him and she wondered why Scott tolerated such brutishness. She assumed that Jorge's one saving grace—his actor's looks—were what kept that relationship going. Then what did that say about Scott? Wouldn't that be just a bit shallow on his part?

At this point of the story you are likely thinking: Oh, Alma and Scott will go into the house and see that it has been burgled. And of course, the box holding the six marbles will be missing. And this event could be read as some sort of metaphor for this or that or the other thing. Because that is the way you have been taught to read short stories. But I will not give you that satisfaction. I have better things to do with my time. I really do. For example, my son wants me to go with him to buy some Chinese food for dinner. My wife is upstairs on the phone with a friend and wants us to get her usual: broccoli beef and steamed rice. If you feel cheated, get over it. Worse things happen in life. Really, they do. I promise.

Better Than Divorce

The bull terrier watched the Lexus fishtail and then straighten as it sped away. The dog turned, looked down, and gently licked his master's forehead.

Elizondo Returns Home

When I first met Elizondo, he lived in the small house at the back end of my abuela's property. Ana Ortiz Camacho, my grandmother and the only grandparent I had the opportunity to know, had died the week before, a life of cigarettes and Mexican food and hard work and not a little beer finally catching up with her. My mother, Abuela's only child, died seven years ago when I was in my senior year at Reed College, so it fell on me to make the funeral arrangements and then begin the arduous task of emptying out Abuela's house and selling it.

It is at a time such as this that I realize how solitary our lives have been. Abuela's husband disappeared so long ago that no one felt the compunction to even mention him by name anymore. And my biological father was some unknown male who sold his sperm to a bank—we know he was (or is) "Hispanic" (the terminology used on the form he filled out) with a college degree and no known cases of cancer or other dreaded diseases in his gene pool. Oh, and he had (or has) an IQ of 136. And me, I'm perpetually single despite being what some might call a good-looking youngish woman with a dream job of assistant professor in the Chicana and Chicano Studies Department at Cal State Northridge where I teach Queer Latina/o Poetics. I can't seem to keep a woman in my bed for longer than six months. Loners, all of us. And now that Abuela has passed on I am more alone than ever.

Anyway, I'd thought the back house was vacant, used more as a storage space than anything else. I hadn't been to that part of the property for years—no reason to—and Abuela always kept me in the main house whenever I paid a visit, which was about every month or so. But when I walked down the driveway the day after the funeral, passing the side of the main house, I could see signs of life in that little house in back: a worn but serviceable brown couch on the porch, three small planters of geraniums set perfectly along the porch's wooden railing, a classic Schwinn Men's Cruiser—in beautiful shape—painted bright, shiny red, its two large tires fully inflated and ready for a ride. And the small house itself was in better shape than I'd ever seen it. That old wood-frame structure had never been anything but in need of fresh paint, and here it was, gleaming white with dark green trim.

As I approached, the gravel under my old Converse high tops seemed to grow louder as my apprehension level elevated. It was almost noon and the Valley heat was just getting started. I tightened the grip on my backpack—heavy with two Norton anthologies and a binder full of student papers needing to be graded—getting ready to swing at this mystery man living on Abuela's property. But then he appeared, slowly opening the screen door, drying his hands on a dishtowel, smiling, nodding at me as if in recognition. I had twenty-five pounds on him, easy, so I relaxed. He couldn't have stood more than five feet tall, very thin, a full head of white hair cropped close to his skull. A handsome man with beautiful brown skin, probably sixty or maybe seventy years old. He just stood there waiting for me to come up to the porch. I stopped about three yards from him and waited.

"Ah," he said in a soft, almost singsong voice. "¡La profesora!"

"You know me?" I asked as my stomach tightened.

"Your abuela bragged and bragged about you," he said, not losing his smile. "She showed me your photos many times, especially that one of you with her when you finished your PhD."

I knew the picture, one of my favorites. Abuela usually never smiled, especially for photos, but this time she displayed a huge grin and hugged me so tightly for the camera I thought she was going to break one of my ribs. We're surrounded by other graduates in caps and gowns, excitement all around. She was prouder at that moment than when I graduated from Reed with a double major in Gender Studies and English. Abuela couldn't figure out how I could make a living wage with that. But she realized I was going to be just fine when I told her that I'd landed a tenure track position at CSUN the week before I was awarded my doctorate from UCLA. A steady job at a major university not too far from her home. It didn't matter that her granddaughter's focus was queer Latina lit . . . she loved me and we just didn't discuss it. What did matter was that I was educated and I had a great job, and she showed it in that picture.

"You know me," I said. "But who are you?"

"Elizondo," he said, his smile slowly disappearing. "Your abuela never mentioned me?"

"No, and I didn't see you at the funeral. Were you there? Did I miss you?" I asked more as a challenge than wanting to hear the answers.

With this, he eased himself onto the couch, which let out a groan of ancient springs. Elizondo shook his head and averted his eyes.

"Why not?" I pressed.

He sighed. "Because I am just a tenant and . . ."

"And?"

He turned back to me: "And I could not think of seeing Ana in a coffin."

I shivered, though I'm not certain why. I seldom heard Abuela's name mentioned . . . she was simply Abuela to me. But when this strange man said her name, it carried a meaning beyond anything I knew about her.

"Have you eaten lunch?" he asked.

I wondered if he could hear my stomach rumble. I shook my head.

"Ah!" he said, standing and smiling again. "I'm heating up some lengua in a delicious soup, not too spicy, with little sliced potatoes. There's plenty."

His description of the beef tongue soup made my mouth water and I could feel my stomach do a flip. And I then noticed the wonderful scent of the soup emanating from the little house. I nodded and walked toward him. I figured he was harmless, and I needed some good Mexican food right then in honor of Abuela and to sate my hunger.

He had me sit at the small table in the kitchen. He kept the house very neat with little adornment. Pure efficiency. He moved back and forth, setting my place, filling a large glass with lemonade, ladling soup into my bowl. After he served himself, he sat, smiled, and commenced eating. I did the same.

"This is so good," I said, and I meant it.

"It is Ana's favorite."

He didn't correct himself to change the "is" to "was." And that was fine. I smiled back at him and continued eating as I formulated questions. We ate in contented silence.

When we finished, he refilled our glasses with lemonade and directed us back to the porch. We sat on the couch with about two feet between us and sipped our cool drinks.

"How long have you lived here?" I finally asked.

He thought for a few moments. "It will be ten months tomorrow."

"Do you pay rent?"

"Por supuesto," he said sounding a bit hurt. "I pay three hundred dollars each month, always on time. And I will pay you tomorrow because it is due."

I thought for a moment. Tomorrow was Saturday, the day I figured I would do the actual packing and organizing of Abuela's things. So I could come by and pick up the money and figure out what to do about Elizondo later. I mean, I did not want to become a landlady. I figured that I could sell Abuela's property and use the money for a down payment on a condo so that I wouldn't have to be a renter anymore. But today the goal was to survey Abuela's belongings, try to figure out what needed to be packed up for storage and what should be sold off. I nodded, said that tomorrow was fine, and for some reason laid out my plans for the next two days. He asked if I needed help, but I declined. This was something I wanted to do in private. I finished my lemonade in one big gulp, handed him the glass, and thanked him for the wonderful lunch. I headed back to Abuela's house to begin. I'd done the same for Mom's apartment when she died, so I kind of had a strategy for making it less onerous. I charted out each room, making lists of this and that, and then prioritized. I was always good at planning, turning big projects into manageable bite-sized jobs. Before I knew it, it was almost midnight. I wondered if Elizondo were still awake, but it would have been rude to bother him just for another good meal. So I hopped in my car, found a McDonald's drive-thru, and ordered a chocolate shake and Angus Deluxe for the drive home.

The next morning I pulled up in front of Abuela's house. My trunk and backseat were filled with dozens of flattened packing boxes. But I first wanted to visit Elizondo, let him pay his rent, and maybe accept his offer of help. I could have used the company that day, the reality of Abuela's death finally sinking in. I walked toward the little house in back, my Converses crunching along the gravel. Elizondo had really made it a nice little place, I had to admit. Even though this area of Van Nuys had not yet felt the full force of gentrification, it was getting there, and this property would likely bring a tidy sum. I went up the three steps to the porch and knocked on the screen door. I didn't hear anything. I tried to peer through the screen but couldn't see anything except shadows.

"Hello?" I said. "Elizondo?"

No answer. I opened the screen door slowly and entered the tiny living room. Everything was in place. I called out his name again, checked the kitchen. Nothing. There was only one place left to search, the small bedroom, so I made my way there in a few steps. The door stood ajar. I called his name again. Again no answer. I slowly pushed the door open.

Elizondo lay in bed, fully clothed, on top of a green bedspread, head nestled in a fluffy pillow, arms crossed. His eyes were opened a bit, lifeless and staring up at the ceiling. A diminutive brown bottle sat on the nightstand, empty. As I approached the body I bumped into a small table to my left. I looked down and saw three new hundred-dollar bills neatly lined up, waiting for me. There was a small piece of yellow paper near the bills with some writing on it. I picked it up and read:

Lo siento. Elizondo

And then I noticed them: three women's rings and a small gold wristwatch set neatly by the money. I sighed and looked over to Elizondo. To say he looked peaceful would have been untruthful. In fact, his expression was one of mild surprise—the kind of surprise you experience when you walk in on a parent getting dressed or happen upon two strangers kissing in public. The kind of surprise that is small, commonplace, but in the end significant beyond its size. The kind of surprise I felt just then.

Mamá's Advice

As she stepped into the warm Los Angeles morning, María remembered what her late mother, Concepción, had told her each night at bedtime since María had turned thirteen: "Mija, when you kill a man, you must find the weak spot that all men have and make him suffer pain as he has never suffered before."

At this point Concepción would always lean close, her hot, moist breath smelling of café con leche and cigarettes, to add: "Don't forget to look straight into his eyes when you do it, otherwise his death will have no meaning."

And María, without fail, would always ask her mother, "What will I see in his eyes, Mamá?"

And also without fail, almost as if it were a strange dance that they had rehearsed each night for many years, Concepción would pull back and exclaim: "You will know when you do it right, mija! You will know it as you know your own name."

An hour earlier, María had stood in Rigoberto's den, walls filled with books collected throughout the years, as Rigoberto gently turned the unblemished pages of a rare, inscribed first English translation of Gabriel García Márquez's magnificent novel *One Hundred Years of Solitude*.

"How did you find this?" Rigoberto had asked in amazement, too afraid to lift his eyes from the book lest it disappear into the ether like so much smoke.

María remembered how she had looked down at her Latin American Studies professor, a man three decades her senior, a brilliant man, winner of too many awards, tenured at a prestigious university, a man who preyed on beautiful, promising undergraduate students such as María. She had stood before this man in silence, waiting for him to look up at her, into her eyes, the way he never seemed to do when they were alone in his bedroom. Finally, María's refusal to answer forced this great man of letters to turn his face upward, toward this young woman whom he assumed would be but a titillating footnote in his life.

Their eyes had finally met. María pulled the long, glistening knife from her purse. Rigoberto's eyes widened.

And as she walked down the sidewalk, warmed by the sun, she smiled because she finally understood her mother's advice, fully and completely, as well as she knew her own name.

Like Rivera and Kahlo

Take it, man. Take it. No, it's cool. She's asleep. My Sandy. Sandy Lerman. Isn't she beautiful? So take the picture of us before she wakes up. I'll leave my sunglasses on because that's how she likes me. Says I look like a real artist. But she's the great artist, really. We're like Rivera and Kahlo. Frida was more immediate, man, totally *there* with her painting. Powerful, all of her pain right up close for all to see. And Diego Rivera knew it. I know it, too, with my Sandy. She's the one with the soul. I totally believe it, man.

Where? Up north for this small art festival. I don't mind bus rides. And Sandy just likes to snooze or sketch the scenery so she doesn't mind either. Yeah, right now she's snoozing, but, man, you should've seen what she did when we left L.A. But snap the picture first. Now. Cool. Thanks, man. Put the camera in my backpack and I'll grab Sandy's sketch pad. Here. Look at this. Can you believe it? She totally captured that dude's face, his raggedy clothes, the shopping cart. Look! Sandy watched him at the bus station for like an hour while we waited for our bus. She just stared at him while he went around picking through trash cans, begging for change, being hassled by the security guard. She watched him, and I swear to God, she drew him in her mind first, and then, when we got on the bus, she just started sketching what she already had in her brain. Too much, man! Too much!

Me? I don't draw like her. No. I take these pictures, see, or I have someone like you, someone I don't know, take a picture with me in it. Then I scan them and manipulate them on my laptop. I'll do that with the picture you took of me and Sandy. I'm going to give it to her. A good-bye gift. What? Well, I'm going to leave her. Decided last week. She doesn't know it yet. I need to find the right time. Maybe when we get there. I don't know, man, I don't know. Need my space, I guess. I'm no good for her anyway. She'd paint and draw way more if she didn't worry about me. Don't get me wrong. I totally love my Sandy. She's everything to me.

But I'm dragging her down. Down. It's best for her, man. If Rivera had left Kahlo, man, Frida would have produced so much more. But she took care of her Diego like he was a baby. No. It's totally for the best, man. No question in my mind. None whatsoever. That bell has been rung, as my mom used to say.

But isn't she beautiful, man? My Sandy. I love to watch her sleep. She's going to love what I do with that picture. Thanks, man. You helped me out big time. You're cool, man. Cool. So why are you going up north? I have this fascination with other people's stories. Lay it on me, man. Lay it on me.

The Lost Soul of Humberto Reyes

Early one Tuesday morning, Isabel Ocampo signed for a package and observed that the return address belonged to her ex-lover, Humberto Reyes. She assumed Humberto had sent yet another exotic trinket he had purchased on one of his many excursions to foreign lands. For despite ending their three-decade romance two years ago, Humberto still adored Isabel and could not help remembering her when he wandered through distant mercados, bazaars, and souks. Isabel found this particular habit of Humberto's somewhat annoying, though also a tad flattering.

Isabel placed the package on her fireplace mantel and proceeded to forget about it for a full day. The next morning, as she drank her first of what would eventually be three cups of very strong, black Cuban coffee (which she preferred despite being Mexican), Isabel saw the package sitting quietly across the room. She sighed, wondered what Humberto found for her this time, and brought the package to the dining room table so that she could continue drinking her coffee.

After she carefully removed the thick, brown paper of the type that Humberto always used to wrap gift boxes, Isabel lifted the note and read. Such notes usually told the story of how Humberto stumbled upon the contents of the box related in such a way that conveyed both pure, unadorned luck combined with incredible cunning and genius. But not this time. Isabel read the note. And she read it again. She blinked, coughed, looked at the package and then back to the note, which she read a third time. In his elegant hand Humberto had written:

> Mi amor, I hope this finds you well. I returned from New Zealand three days ago, but by the time you receive this I will be in transit to a place I would rather not disclose, at least not at this time. While I am away (which should be no longer than a week), I ask you to protect what I have placed

into this box. What is it? Well, to be blunt (something I attempt to avoid in my daily interactions, as you know), I have put my soul into this box for safekeeping. Why? I am afraid that I will lose it during my travels. I will explain more fully when (and if) I return. Con abrazos, Humberto.

Isabel opened the box and sure enough, there was her ex-lover's soul resting on a bed of purple velvet. She had expected something a bit larger, perhaps more Byzantine in appearance. But there it sat, a soul nonetheless. Isabel closed the box and shook her head. "Damn him," she whispered. "Damn him."

Seven days later Humberto appeared on Isabel's doorstep. To her eye he looked ten, maybe fifteen years younger. Humberto had lost weight but not in a sickly manner, in a way that made him look vigorous, youthful. Isabel let him in and poured two small glasses of sweet wine. After a bit of small talk and cheerful laughter, Humberto suddenly grew serious. He sat up in his chair and leaned toward Isabel.

"May I have my soul back?"

Isabel took a sip of wine and looked away.

"What do you mean?" she asked, keeping her eyes trained on the crackling flames in the fireplace.

Humberto let out a sound that was not quite human, a cross between a hum and a scream. He collected himself and asked again: "May I have my soul back?"

Isabel did not answer and kept her eyes on the blazing logs.

Finally, after what seemed years to Humberto, Isabel answered: "Isn't the fire lovely? It has never looked more beautiful."

@chicanowriter

Xiaojing gags as Tenorio sets the faded Los Angeles Zoo coffee mug on his placemat near hers. She quickly covers her mouth, stands, and runs to the powder room by the hallway closet. As she wretches, bathroom door wide open, Tenorio stifles a laugh as he remembers when they had their first long conversation after a panel at a writers' conference and she said her name meant "morning luxuriance." Not so much these days. A full month of morning sickness with no end in sight. Tenorio's late wife, Renata, suffered maybe a total of seven or eight days of nausea for her pregnancy with the twins, something Tenorio made the mistake of mentioning to Xiaojing two weeks ago. Her response: She was perfect, right? For a poet, Xiaojing could be blunt.

The gagging stops. Water runs. Xiaojing gargles with mouthwash and spits, returns to the breakfast table.

Can I get you anything, sweetheart? Tenorio asks softly, oozing husbandly tenderness, concern.

You can drink your coffee someplace else, she says. You know I can't stand the smell right now.

Tenorio tries to smile but it looks like he's just bitten the inside of his cheek. He puts the newspaper down, picks up his iPhone with one hand, the coffee mug with the other, softly kisses the top of Xiaojing's head, and shuffles in his slippers to the living room. Once there, he puts his cup down on the *Dead Sea Scrolls* coffee table book and settles onto the couch.

Use a coaster! Xiaojing yells from the other room. I did, he yells back and waits, doesn't move. After four long seconds: No you didn't, she responds in a loud, exhausted whisper. Yes I did, he coos. Silence. Tenorio sighs, reaches for a Beatles coaster—the one with a miniature copy of the *Revolver* cover—places it on the *Dead Sea Scrolls* book near his coffee mug, and ever so slowly, silently moves his mug onto the coaster. Thank you, Xiaojing yells. I appreciate it. Tenorio sighs.

Just over two years ago, Tenorio moderated a panel at the AWP conference titled *Cultural Edifices: Writers of Color in Today's Literary Marketplace*. It was a solid panel, one he'd planned for almost a year, but three weeks before the conference his old friend, novelist Henry Leong, came down with pneumonia, a nasty case, and had to drop out. Henry recommended Xiaojing as a replacement. Tenorio wasn't certain if she'd be a good fit. He already had one Cuban poet and one African American poet. Henry along with the fourth panelist, a Native American memoirist, had created a more or less balanced panel: two poets, two prose writers. But Tenorio had little choice. He called Xiaojing, explained the situation, mentioned Henry, and she accepted without hesitation. Said she'd be honored. Xiaojing turned out to be the hit of the panel, a beautiful young poet who could be lyrical one moment, hilariously blunt the next. That night, after a reception that served too much free booze and too little food, Tenorio and Xiaojing disappeared into her hotel room. They missed the next day's panel presentations put on by their friends and colleagues, lounging in bed, enjoying each other's bodies. She didn't mind that he was almost fifty with all the scars and discolorations that come with age. Indeed, the fact that he had lived twenty years longer than she, twenty years of experience that included a late wife and twins at Stanford, pleased her deeply, at least that's what she told him at the end of the conference when they had to separate and fly out of Chicago to their respective California cities. They promised to keep in touch. Xiaojing even hinted that she was growing weary of San Diego and wanted to move to Los Angeles where the poetry scene (not to mention teaching opportunities) was vibrant, especially for a Chinese American writer. Before Tenorio knew it they were married and living in his Sherman Oaks ranch-style house, the one he had bought with Renata on the money she made as a partner at a large downtown law firm. The house that made a perfect place to raise the twins. The house Renata died in, eventually succumbing to ovarian cancer. The house he had promised Renata to keep and to share with a future new wife. A promise he never intended to keep but would eventually fulfill, despite feeling like a traitor to his first marriage. But Tenorio said to Renata that he would never have another child with the new wife. Never. This made Renata smile. She died one month later, in their bed, made comfortable with a cocktail of painkillers, no need to fear addiction.

Tenorio takes a sip of coffee, puts the mug back on the coaster, turns on the iPhone, and goes to his Twitter page. What to share? Hmmmmm . . . oh, yes:

Tenorio Moreno @chicanowriter
Reading review copy of Michael Nava's new novel "The
City of Palaces." Gr8!

There, he thinks. My 768 followers will know that Nava has a new book
coming out soon. Tenorio stares at his tweet, waiting for someone to
retweet it, or at least Favorite it. Nothing. Well, how about this, something
a bit more confrontational, something involving a hot-button issue that
will entice the trolls:

Tenorio Moreno @chicanowriter
Thought-provoking piece in The American Scholar
(@TheAmScho):
Leaving Race Behind by @AmitaiEtzioni
http://theamericanscholar.org/leaving-race-behind/

Tenorio sends the tweet, waits, stares at his iPhone. One minute. Two.
Nothing. He snorts, places the iPhone on the *Dead Sea Scrolls,* gulps down
the rest of his coffee, yells over to Xiaojing: I think I'll go to the gym before
I start writing.

She answers: Sounds like a plan.

Kind of stuck on that short story, he adds. Need to get the juices
flowing.

She answers: I said it sounds like a plan.

It's a plan, he says to himself. A real, solid, well-constructed, fucking
plan.

Tenorio tries to read the advance copy of the Nava novel as he pedals on
the recumbent stationary bike. Some of his best story ideas came to him
while he was at the gym reading other people's fiction. Maybe something
will come to Tenorio now. But no. A man about Tenorio's age is on the bike
to his left, yakking on his cell phone despite the strict gym prohibition. It's
in writing, right up there on the wall, for Christ's sake! Motherfucker. And
he has to talk loud enough so that anyone within a three-yard radius will
know that he's a surgeon offering advice to a friend about who would be
the best doctor to see for a hip replacement. Not an emergency. No need

to have that call right then. Motherfucker. Wait! That's it! thinks Tenorio. I'll have my main character go to the gym, get annoyed by a doctor who's yakking into a cell phone. Describe the doctor in superb, craftsmanlike detail. Good set piece, nice bridge to the next scene where he'll have an epiphany about his life while driving home. Yes! That could work nicely. God bless you, Dr. Motherfucker! God bless you and your fucking cell phone!

———————

Tenorio enters his house through the attached garage. I'm home, sweetie! he yells. He doesn't see Xiaojing in the kitchen or living room or dining room. No answer, but he can hear the shower running upstairs. He almost skips up the stairs, anxious to take his own shower and then get down to writing. Tenorio enters their bedroom, knocks on the bathroom door. Sweetie, I'm home, he says. No answer. Sweetie? he says again. You okay?

After a few moments, before Tenorio panics and opens the door, Xiaojing yells from the shower: Is that you, honey?

Tenorio relaxes. Yes, sweetie. Can I come in?

Sure.

Tenorio opens the door and looks at Xiaojing through the steamed glass shower door. He wants to say something but instead he takes in the view of his pregnant second wife.

Good workout? Xiaojing finally asks as she works lather into her hair.

Yes, sweetie, says Tenorio. Yes, I had a great workout.

Your knees feel okay?

Tenorio laughs softly. Oh, yes, he says. Never felt better.

Xiaojing rinses her hair, shuts off the water. Tenorio turns, walks out of the bathroom before Xiaojing can step out of the shower, slowly closing the door behind him.

Xiaojing yells: You okay?

Yes, answers Tenorio as he walks to the study, giving up on taking a shower for now. Like a million bucks, he yells over his shoulder. Like a million bucks.

———————

After a few minutes of writing sentences that make sense, that sing, that move his short story forward, he hits that black wall of his. Nothing. For the last twenty minutes he has stared at the blinking cursor, waiting for the flood to begin again.

Tenorio shakes his head. A sound, loud, not quite human, breaks into his consciousness. What is that? Who is that? Xiaojing? Her screams splinter Tenorio's concentration. He jumps from his chair, trips, almost falls to the carpet. Xiaojing? What's wrong?

Tenorio opens the bathroom door. His wife sits in the corner, on the cold tile, bath towel open, legs spread, a pool of red bubbling out of her. She screams again.

As Tenorio moves to her, arms outstretched, a loving husband trying to help his wife, he tries to capture this image of his beautiful woman's face contorted in fear and pain, capture it in his still-agile memory, keep this image and every detail for safekeeping to draw upon at the appropriate time to write a heartrending section of his short story, a piece of fiction that will finally make him an A-lister, a writer's writer, a man to be reckoned with.

The King of Lighting Fixtures

1.

Empire.

David Rey liked the word, the way it rolled off his tongue, filled his mind with images of Alexander the Great and shields and armor and conquered lands.

Empire.

His empire.

True, the *Los Angeles Times* article misstated a few basic facts, such as David's age, making him two years younger than his true age of forty. And the writer misquoted him ever so slightly. When asked how it felt to oversee a business empire, one of the most successful chains of lighting fixture stores in California, David Rey *had* answered: "All it takes is a lot of hard work and a little luck." The reporter mistakenly wrote it as: "All it takes is a little hard work and a lot of luck."

No matter. In fact, the error made David seem a bit humble, as if his great empire arose from God's good graces rather than the sweat of his brow. That's humility. That's good press. That's what makes America great. But the word used by the reporter—empire—transformed the article into something extraordinary. What a perfect, muscular word. *Empire.* Yes. *The Empire Strikes Back!* A Hollywood dream. That's what David Rey was doing: living a dream with stores spanning California from San Diego to Sacramento, a baker's dozen in all. Pretty good for not finishing college. Now these young, eager graduates from Stanford and USC and Loyola Marymount and virtually all of the UC campuses worked for him—David wanted only the best and the brightest as his managers and accountants and lawyers.

The woman, no . . . girl, really—she was not a fully developed woman yet, at least not by David's view of things—snored a bit and turned ever so slightly. David brought the *Los Angeles Times* down from his face so he could admire her, asleep and almost swallowed up by his rumpled sheets, the sign of a good night of fun. David shifted in the loveseat, admired this girl across the bedroom, about half his age (a college student for God's sake!) who wanted to go home with him rather than with any of those impoverished, embryonic boys who might have him on youth, but not on class, not on money, and certainly not on manhood. Those punks had no pinche empire, that's for goddamn sure. ¡Pendejos!

He had seen that face before last night but couldn't remember where. At a restaurant or the CVS or Albertsons. He shook his head. It'd come to him. But more important, what was her name? He took a sip of coffee, blinked, and gathered his thoughts. Think, think. Why did female names slip from his mind so easily? Think. Yes! Bat. Bat Blanco. Call me Batty, she'd said as she accepted David's offer to buy her another Red Bull Passion Slush at the TGI Friday's on Canoga Avenue. Patrons crowded around the boisterous bar cheering as the Lakers opened up a lead. As David sipped his Heineken with one eye on the flat screen and one on Bat, she said that her real name was Bertha but that sounded like an old, worn-out name. Not a good fit for this petite young woman. She promised to tell David how she came to that new name, but he'd have to wait, be a patient chico. Unfortunately, patience was not one of David Rey's attributes. And he had no intention of allowing this pleasant diversion to last more than a week, maybe two at most. He'd been married once, long ago, but ended it when it became clear that she—Ramona—didn't really believe in David and his dreams for something better, something beyond what most people could imagine, and would have been happy with a nine-to-five husband who was there for dinner each night, fathering three, four, or maybe five babies, mowing the lawn each Saturday, attending Mass on Sunday, a belly growing larger by the year. Forget about building an empire, hombre. Settle down, make a home, produce children. That's what Ramona dreamed of, nothing less, and certainly nothing more.

No. David Rey figured that he'd never know why Bertha renamed herself Bat due to the consistency of his internal dating calendar. But such is life. Bat brought some delight to David's workaday existence, made him feel young for a short while, and that was that. As David hardened his heart, Bat started to stir. She turned this way and that, her thin, brown arms tossing above her head like those of a rag doll being swung by a reckless toddler—beautiful arms seemingly animated by the power of an unseen other.

"Batty?" said David.

Bat blinked three times and then sat up quickly—too fast for one who had just been asleep, or so it seemed to David. The sheet fell to her waist. David took in a deep breath, remembering suddenly that he'd been inside this stunning young woman just a few hours ago, her thin but strong legs trapping him tight and secure, a delightful prison.

Bat focused on David's face for a few seconds. She smiled and turned to the clock on the nightstand. Then her smile fell away.

"¡Chingao!" Bat yelped as she scrambled out of bed almost falling face first onto the thick wall-to-wall carpet.

David stood, his robe falling open, but he didn't care because he knew he looked lean.

"What?" said David.

"Work!"

"It's Saturday," he said before remembering that many people, of course, worked on the weekend including his own salespeople and staff.

Bat ran to the bathroom but didn't close the door. David could hear her pee, loud and clear. Flush. More mad scrambling, and then the shower started with a wet *whoosh!* David marveled at how Bat made herself at home so quickly.

Saturday. David had worked many a Saturday, but no longer. Sure, he might drop in on one of his stores, maybe the one closest to home in Woodland Hills or a bit farther east in Encino or maybe a longish drive on the freeway out to Koreatown or Glendale or Simi Valley. He liked to see his managers hop to, their eyes almost popping out of their skulls at the surprise visit by El Jefe. They were a conscientious lot, that's for sure. David handpicked his managers, always offering the top salaries and most comprehensive health packages in the lighting business, easily outbidding his competitors. He wanted the best, nothing less, because David knew that money spent in the right places on the right people would lead to success. He didn't need any pinche MBA to know this. If David had anything, he had common sense. He'd used it to great advantage in starting his first lighting fixture store in Koreatown not more than a mile from the house he had shared with his mother and four younger sisters. David's father would have been proud, no doubt, with the opening of that one shop. But sometimes he wondered what Osvaldo would have thought of the ribbon cutting at the thirteenth store, this one way up in Sacramento. David's father had worked his whole life with his hands, first in the fields when he and his young bride, Elisa, had left Mexico and settled in Oxnard. After David was born they moved to Los Angeles, and Osvaldo immediately started his manic routine of juggling two city jobs—as a janitor in a high-rise, a valet parking attendant wearing a red vest at yet another—just so his wife could be home with baby David and the eventual succession of daughters. Elisa had warned her husband—thirty pounds too heavy and suffering from hypertension—that he'd work himself into an early grave. And she was right. One of the other parking attendants grew worried after Osvaldo had been away too long from their station and went searching for him on level two of the vast underground parking garage. He finally found Osvaldo sitting in a Jaguar XKR-S convertible coupe, behind the wheel after parking it in space number 243, not ten yards from the elevator, looking as if he decided to close his eyes for but a moment, head nestled in the soft, black leather headrest. The only thing missing was lovely music, perhaps a little Vivaldi or maybe a bit of Chopin, emanating from the Jaguar's speakers. Osvaldo's life ended in elegance even though it was not his own. But if he could see his son's success now, what would he think? Would he swell with pride? Would he call his family in Mexico to brag about David living the American Dream? Yes, of course he would, all of that and more. His only son had made the family wealthy and treated his mother to a four-bedroom, two-and-a-half-bath, newly remodeled home in Sherman Oaks, with two of his four sisters coming back to the nest—one from a nasty, childless marriage and the other from a failed suicide attempt but doing much better. Elisa could mother these two daughters in great comfort. Osvaldo would have patted David on his back, speechless. That's how a man takes care of his family.

"Can I use your deodorant?"

David jumped. He'd been so lost in thought he hadn't realized that Bat had finished her shower and was scuttling about the bedroom in blue panties and black bra. The mismatch made him smile.

"Oh, sure, it's in the medicine cabinet."

Bat scampered back to the bathroom. David listened as Bat rummaged through the cabinet's contents. She let out a little chuckle. What was so funny? She finally emitted a dramatic *aha!* David approached and watched as Bat pulled the top off his Right Guard Sports Stick and sniffed.

"A manly man scent," she said and applied it quickly under each arm. "Muy macho."

"No one could confuse you for a man, mija," said David.

The moment "mija" left his lips, he cringed. Rule number one: never call a new, younger lover "my daughter."

Bat smiled, ran to the side of the bed, and found her black skirt. She held it up and shrugged. "A few wrinkles never hurt anyone, right, papi?"

David cringed again. Why had he called her mija? God. And now she teased him by calling him "papi."

Bat found her short boots, slipped into them, and deftly zipped each one. She poked around the crumpled sheets and found her black Calvin Klein V-neck sweater. Bat pulled it over her head, pushed up both sleeves to the elbow, then posed with hands on hips, chin tucked down, looking very much like a model in a Macy's catalog.

"Good as new!" she finally chirped.

David walked up to Bat but didn't touch her.

"Much better, yes," he said. "But I didn't mind you without the clothes."

She curtsied and said: "Mil gracias, papi."

"Don't call me 'papi,'" said David.

"No time for small talk, papi, gotta pay the bills." She suddenly stopped moving and looked up to the ceiling as if a memory took over her thoughts. "I need to wash my hands."

Before David could say anything, Bat ran back to the bathroom and shut the door behind her. Odd. She didn't mind peeing and showering with the door wide open, but she had to wash her hands in private. What a peculiar girl. The water shut off and Bat emerged, grinning at some private joke. She jogged to the dresser, grabbed her purse, allowed David to give her a peck on the cheek, and trotted toward the bedroom door.

"Need a ride?"

Bat kept moving forward. "No, it's close by, just a few blocks away on Ventura. There's a bus stop at the corner. And I have a bus pass, all bought and paid for!"

"Where do you work?"

Bat was already down the stairs making her way toward the front door. David followed helplessly, pulling his robe closed.

"A few blocks away, I told you!"

Bat opened the front door and looked up toward David at the top of the stairs.

"See you, papi," she said as she slammed the door behind her.

David slowly took three steps down, not quite knowing what had just happened. Usually there was small talk with these women he brought home, maybe a little breakfast, some gentle whisperings acknowledging the intimacy shared, but a firm, unspoken acceptance of the transitory nature of the previous night's romance.

But this woman—this girl—this Bat, was an unknowable whirlwind. ¡Ay! David never had such an encounter, such an odd good-bye. Then David's mind started to whir: a few blocks away someplace on Ventura Boulevard. But where exactly? What was open this early on Saturday? The Ralphs supermarket? No, David couldn't see Bat stocking shelves, arranging tomatoes, bananas, blueberries, and grapes, or working the cash register. Jerry's Famous Deli? Maybe. But not quite right. No, not for Bat, but maybe. Ah! That coffee house, what was it called? Not Starbucks, but some independent place where Pierce College students liked to nurse a cup of coffee for hours while doing schoolwork. David didn't mind the place. In fact, he'd had more than his share of coffees there with Nate Klayman, the manager of his Woodland Hills store. Is that where he'd seen Bat before? Maybe. That coffee house would be a perfect place for an unusually beautiful and clever college student to work. But how did she get to the bar last night? Did she really take the bus? Did she live in one of those small new apartments in Woodland Hills? Did Bat share rent with another cute college student? College student. God, he *was* old enough to be Bat's papi. No matter. Maybe after a long, hot shower, David would drop by and order a latte and a blueberry scone. Would Bat register any level of surprise? She'd have to ask him his name, write it on the side of the cup. Would she remember? Or would Bat write "Papi" with a little happy face added to make a point? What point?

David walked back to his bedroom and surveyed the battlefield. He could still feel Bat's presence, her energy. And he could sniff out her scent. David slowly strolled around the room, neatening up after this young, wild thing. He moved to the bathroom and shook his head. Bat had simply dropped her wet towel on the floor, just like that, without a worry. Is this how young people act in someone else's home? He picked it up and observed several strands of her long, black hair coiled in the towel's folds. David dropped it dramatically into the wicker hamper shaking his head like a disappointed parent. Then he remembered that Bat had laughed when she opened his medicine cabinet. David opened it and peered in— nothing odd, not an embarrassing thing in sight. He closed it and chalked it up to Bat's clearly eccentric personality.

But then he saw it: Bat had written four words on the steamed mirror of the medicine cabinet. When did she do that? Ah, that's why she washed her hands in private. Sneaky little one, that's for sure. He read the words: EYES OF A BLUE DOG. They made no sense, none at all. Bat had written them quickly. Some kind of weird joke. A *young* joke on an old man. She mocked him, no doubt. But so what? He'd made no commitment to her, just had a little fun for the night. David reached up with his right hand, palm out, and reread the words one more time before wiping them away with a flurry of irritated squeaks.

2.

Interview with Ramona

Q: How long were you and David married?

A: Oh, not long. (*Sighs.*) Not even two years.

Q: I'm sorry, is this difficult for you? We could do it another time if you wish.

A: No, that's okay. It's been about twenty years since the divorce so the pain isn't so bad. It's just sometimes I get sad about what could have been. You know how that is, don't you?

Q: Well . . .

A: Probably not. You're still young and pretty.

Q: No, that's not it . . .

A: I was young once, and beautiful if that doesn't sound all conceited.

Q: No, you're still beautiful.

A: Gracias. But not so young, right? Though I have kept my figure, even after three babies. I married again after David, you know. Russell. Not such a bad guy. Works at the Honda dealership on Topanga. One of their best salesmen.

Q: Yes, all that is in my notes here someplace . . .

A: Ni modo. Anyway, David couldn't get enough of me. It was like he was so thirsty and all he wanted was to drink from me, from my body.

Q: How did you meet?

A: (*Laughs.*) I worked in the bookstore at Pierce College,

you know, that community college in Woodland Hills. A cashier. My first real job where I could keep most of my paycheck since I moved out on my own when my parents said it was time for me to be an adult. I was seventeen.

Q: David was a student, right?

A: Yes. He was eighteen. And you think he's handsome now, you should have seen him then! Want to see a picture of us? I keep one in my wallet.

Q: After all these years?

A: Some things you have to keep.

Q: I suppose.

A; Russell would be pissed if he knew I had this. Ah, here it is! Look at us. Just babies, really.

Q: Wonderful!

A: Look at that hair I had!

Q: May I borrow this? I'd love to make a copy.

A: No, this is private.

Q: But you agreed to the interview.

A: Only the interview. This picture is private. It's a little bit of me. I don't mind if you see it. But I don't want all the readers to see it, okay?

Q: (*Hands back photograph.*) Fair enough. I understand.

A: I don't think you do. But that's okay. You're young. You don't have regrets. Yet.

Q: (*Coughs.*) So, you met David when he was buying books for his classes?

A: No, actually, it was when I took a smoke break. Outside the bookstore, by the side of the building. That's where we always took our breaks, me, the people who worked at the bookstore and the little coffee shop nearby. A couple of us were able to take our fifteen minutes at the same time. I'd seen him in the bookstore before that, browsing but not buying, which was kind of funny because classes had already started. I don't know if he ever bought his books. We noticed each other but never spoke. But that one day when I was taking my break, I'm talking with my friend Carla who worked in the coffee shop and we see David walking toward the bookstore. Carla says something like she wouldn't mind having a little bit of him and I laugh because she could just speak her mind and not be ashamed or anything the way I would if I did that. I heard she died a couple of years ago. Boyfriend went off on her. It was in the news, on TV. He killed himself after. But I hadn't seen Carla in something like twenty years. She's still young in my mind. Young, chubby, cute. So David is walking in our direction and sees me and Carla. He slows down just before the stairs up to the bookstore, turns in our direction. Carla and me just giggle, you know, because we're kids, really, and David was so handsome and looked older than eighteen, more like three or four years older because he lifted weights and was filled out like a man, not like the other guys on campus. So he slowly walks up to us, shields his eyes from the sun with his right hand, and his muscles on his arm kind of flex in a special way, like soft, brown waves, and he smiles and says: "What's your name?" That was it. I knew we'd be together after that.

Q: Love at first sight?

A: (*Laughs.*) Love? I never said anything about love. Love doesn't exist. At least, not for people like me.

Q: People like you?

A: You know, ordinary people.

Q: (*Looks at watch.*) Oh, could we meet again? I have more questions, but I have to call Olivas.

A: The guy writing this story?

Q: Yes. A real pendejo.

A: (*Laughs.*) No worries. Just call when you want to talk some more. It feels good to talk to someone about David.

Q: You're a doll, thanks.

A: Tell that to my husband.

3.

Bat leapt off the bus, almost stumbling onto the pavement, but she quickly regained her balance. She let out a little snort, then broke into a trot, keeping her eyes trained on the coffee house's large hanging sign, bold brown lettering on an orange background: LOT 49. Bat pushed the glass door, entered the shop, took three steps, and stopped before moving deeper into the long room. She quickly scanned the place: from behind one of the two cash registers Serge smiled and exchanged inane and insincere pleasantries with a customer, Dean wiped a table in the back near the restrooms, and Leonard scooped dark, shiny coffee beans into the Bunn grinder. Only three patrons stood in line. Not so bad. But where was Miles, the manager? Bat moved her eyes back and forth, keeping her head still so that no one would notice her panic. Miles, where are you? He was always here, even when nursing a cold. Maybe he's in the restroom.

"Looking for someone?"

Bat tried not to jump, attempted to stay cool, as she slowly turned to her left. She almost succeeded in conveying the insouciance of an innocent woman.

"Miles," she cooed. "Mi jefe. ¿Qué onda, hombre?"

Miles stared at Bat as he stood frozen, stooped over the newspaper holder—a V-shaped container made of shiny metal mesh sold by IKEA—hands full of newsprint, midway through taking care one of his pet peeves: messy newspapers and magazines dropped into the holder by patrons who didn't mind sharing their discards with other customers but had less of a sense of order than Lot 49's morning shift manager. "Mr. OCD" his staff called him behind his back. But it made him a better manager in many ways, a neurosis he channeled into making the coffee house hum along with by-the-book barista training and regular refresher courses, not to mention mandatory clockwork emptying of waste containers, floor swabbing, tabletop wiping, and restroom disinfecting. Bat believed Miles was not bad looking, sort of a young, thin, blond Alec Baldwin, and he'd majored in philosophy at CSUN so he had a brain, actually quite a good one, and could discuss Kierkegaard, Nietzsche, Camus, Sartre, and Heidegger with the ease most men his age chatted about tattoos, PlayStation 3, getting fucked up, and the Dodgers. Bat's growing desire to minor in philosophy was fanned when Miles went on about metaphysics, the nature of the mind and freedom, existential psychoanalysis. She'd read *The Stranger* three times because Miles told her—in his convincing way—that it was a book that went deeper into what it means "to be" than any other book, even the Bible. Bat wondered if Miles was straight or gay, which annoyed her since she usually could figure it out within a minute of meeting a man. But at this moment, Bat's existence depended on smoothing over her tardiness with Mr. OCD.

"So, our UCLA student has been enjoying her nightlife passions just a bit too much to make it to her—what is this?—oh, yes, *job*—on time?"

Uh-oh. Whenever Miles referred to Bat's university he was really pissed. She knew that he could not afford to attend UCLA, despite getting in, and that despite really *liking* Bat, he felt she was not taking full advantage of all UCLA had to offer, especially since she was a Chicano Studies major. "What is this, the 1970s?" he'd mocked when first learning of Bat's area of study. "Should I yell, 'Attica, Attica, Attica!' whenever you come into Lot 49?" Bat had to go to Wikipedia to understand what Miles meant. She first ended up in the article that explained that Attica was a historical region of Greece that included Athens, that country's current capital. This made no sense. But she clicked around a bit and found the article on the Attica Correctional Facility in Attica, New York. Okay, a prison riot ignited by the death of a black radical activist. Political radicalism. People of color. Got it. Point made.

Bat took two steps toward Miles, stopped, shrugged, and offered an almost inaudible, "Sorry." She tried to make her eyes moisten, did her best to look pathetic, but failed.

Miles turned back to arranging the newspapers and magazines. He shook his head in barely hidden disgust. This was not going to be a good day at Lot 49, at least not for Bat. She went to the back room, put on her brown apron and matching cap, grabbed a damp washcloth, and trotted back to start wiping down the already clean tables. She approached a table near the entryway, where she could see pedestrians strolling along the sunny but cool sidewalks of Ventura Boulevard, envying their idleness, wishing she could enjoy her Saturdays without having to work as many hours as Miles was willing to give her to pay for tuition and books and rent. Financial aid was not enough. She took the bus whenever she could to save on gas and prolong the life of her 1999 Honda Civic. Bat kept her small, low-rent apartment in Canoga Park (*Woodland Hills adjacent!* proclaimed the ad) rather than search for an even smaller place at four times the rent near UCLA. That way, too, she could be close to her mother and two little brothers, who lived in a little wood-frame house on Victory Boulevard about six blocks from Bat's apartment. Her mother sometimes needed help with the boys, especially when she had to work the night shift at Target. Bat even scrimped by keeping a prehistoric Motorola RAZR flip phone that made her classmates laugh as they whipped out their latest iPhones. She didn't even own a TV but didn't have time to watch anyway. So Bat resented feeling guilty over having a fun night of drinks and sex. She was human, after all. What's wrong with a little "passion" every now and then, even if her private life was a little bit complicated? Certainly an existentialist such as Miles could understand that, right?

Bat finished wiping the table and turned to do another, and almost ran her forehead into Miles' narrow chest. She looked up and noticed that his face was smooth with a clean shave. Bat admired the dimple on his chin that must have been difficult to keep clear of whiskers it was so deep.

"Yes, mi jefe?"

"Can we talk, Bat?"

"Sure, of course, anything for you, Miles."

"In the managers' office."

Miles never said "my office" because he shared it with the night manager, Kavita Lankesh-Williams. Bat assumed that Miles was incapable of ignoring the fact that someone else had the right to use this space. This was particularly appropriate since Kavita was not only ten years his senior but also had been only the second manager hired by the owners of Lot 49 when it opened seven years ago. True, Miles now had three solid years' experience as manager—after being a star barista for two—but he very openly respected seniority. Soon he'd have enough money to buy a small townhouse or condo, maybe find a more intellectually gratifying job, and perhaps even consider applying to graduate school. But for now he followed the rules, worked hard, and honored the pecking order.

Miles entered the managers' office first and quickly sat behind the elegant Danish modern teak desk. As Bat started to lower herself into one of the two guest chairs, Miles said, "Please close the door."

Chingao. This is not good.

Bat complied and then sat. She figured the best thing to do was to let Miles take the lead, let him begin with a little speech about how lucky Bat was to have a job in this economy, that when Miles hired her last year, forty-two people had submitted applications ahead of hers, and almost all were overqualified. Miles had given this lecture before, but he seemed particularly angry this morning. The air conditioner blew hard and cold right above Bat's head, so she sat on her hands and tried not to shiver, as if shivering were a sign of weakness she could not afford to exhibit. Behind Miles hung a large Lot 49 framed poster that consisted of an extreme close-up of a single shiny, deep brown coffee bean with the coffee house's motto *No Better Coffee . . . We Mean It!* in white lettering along the bottom border. Very little else decorated the office. The shelves held some generic books on coffee as well as several Lot 49 manager manuals, a new one issued each year. Only one item stood out: on the desk sat a small, blue ceramic dog with shiny black eyes. This made Bat smile and feel safe. She let out a little chuckle.

"Something amusing?"

"I like your dog."

"It's not mine, it belongs to Kavita," said Miles as he scratched at his chin. He added: "It's silly if you ask me."

The blue dog stared at Bat with its black eyes. It was like the one in her strange, vague dream of last night—though she and David slept very little—the inspiration for the five words she wrote on David's bathroom mirror this morning. She still couldn't figure out the significance of it, particularly since she had no belief in the magic of dreams the way her grandmother did.

"It's new?" she asked.

"Yes," said Miles who now closed his eyes as if staving off a migraine. "Feel free to take it if you wish."

Bat blinked.

"Just joking," Miles quickly added when he realized Bat might actually snatch up the ceramic dog. "It's obviously not mine to give."

Miles opened his eyes and focused on Bat's forehead, which annoyed her each time he did this, usually when Bat had upset him. It reminded Bat of how she felt on Ash Wednesday when non-Catholics would stare at the smudge of flaking black ash just above her brow. On those days she felt like saying: "Do you want to lick it off?"

Miles sat back, steepled his fingers, and began: "You know how lucky you are to have this job?"

Bat sighed and wondered if Miles would stop his little speech if she went around his desk, put her hand on his crotch, and rubbed until he came. Instead, she kept her eyes locked on the blue dog and answered: "Yes, Miles."

"You are my best worker."

Oh, this is a little different, thought Bat. Miles never jumped right into the inevitable compliment this early in his speech.

"Gracias," she said feeling some relief. "And you're a great jefe."

Miles waved her off. "No need to kiss ass."

"But I'm not."

"Let me finish."

Bat lifted her eyes from the blue dog and looked at Miles, who was now staring not at Bat's forehead but at her nose. Baby-step progress. Bat immediately made it her goal to will Miles to look directly into her eyes.

Miles sighed and continued: "I need to take a leave of absence." His eyes now met Bat's, which widened into mini-Frisbees with this announcement.

"How long?"

Miles shifted in his chair and moved his eyes to the blue dog. He smiled. "However long it takes."

Bat cleared her throat, not certain how to react, what to say, not really wanting to know the whys, what fors, and becauses. In movies it was always cancer or some other disease just as horrible.

"I've met a wonderful woman." His eyes shifted up back to Bat, making eye contact again. "She lives in Kansas City. Er, the one in Missouri."

Something about this news made Bat tingle. And she now knew Miles liked women. Well, at least one woman.

"When did you go to Kansas City?"

"Catherine is completing her doctorate in art history at UMKC," Miles continued as if Bat had not asked a question. "She's trying to decide where she wants to apply for teaching jobs. Her ultimate goal is to be a museum curator."

"When did you go to Kansas City?"

"Her focus is Meso-American and Native American arts, so you see, California would be a perfect fit for her, right?"

Ah, he's trying out arguments that he hoped to use on this Catherine of Kansas City, Missouri.

"Yes," said Bat. "Especially Southern California. You know, the Chumash, Tongva. And all of the Southwest did belong to Mexico once."

Miles jumped to his feet, arms raised above his head as if he were about to catch a football. His short sleeves rode up on his biceps, which were better defined than Bat had expected.

"Yes, Bat! That's what I said to Catherine!"

"But when did you go to Kansas City?"

Miles relented, his arms fell to his sides, and he admitted: "We met online about six months ago. I haven't met Catherine in the flesh yet."

But you've seen her naked, for sure, thought Bat. Thank God for Skype.

"So, my plan is to take a couple weeks off of work and visit Catherine. But if I need more time to convince her to consider jobs out here, it might stretch out a bit." And then Miles added, almost as a threat: "I have a lot of vacation time saved up."

Bat didn't like the direction this was headed. She was already stretched thin by school and work and helping her mother with the boys.

"But I can't—," she began.

"I know, I know." Miles waved off Bat's objections. "You're not full time and all that. But I need you, Bat. Could we work something out where you're managing but with the help of . . ."

"Serge or Dean?"

"Yes, Serge or Dean," said Miles a bit relieved. "But not Leonard. Maybe both Serge and Dean could assist you while I'm gone. Like a tag team, but with you in charge. And there would be extra money for you, too, of course."

Bat sat up, her inner mechanism readjusting—click, click, click—like the workings of an antique clock. *He needs me—this is not the usual lecture where he makes me feel like a little girl. I am now his equal.* She cocked her head a bit to the right, pretending to roll his proposal around in her mind.

"May I think about it?" she finally said after counting three beats.

Miles allowed a small smile to creep onto his lips. *Love will find a way,* that smile said. Miles walked to the door and opened it. Bat stood and took a step.

"Yes, of course," he said while keeping his hand on the door handle. "But if you could let me know relatively soon, that would make my life much easier, okay? Talk to your boyfriend about it, if you have to."

Bat stopped. "What?"

"Uri. Talk to him if you need to."

"Why would I do that?"

Miles blinked. "Oh, sorry. I thought you two were still together."

"We are," said Bat. "But he's in Israel visiting his family. Starting a new job when he gets back. I don't want to bother him."

"Oh."

"I can make this decision alone."

Miles nodded.

"I'll do it," she said after a moment. "You've got a deal."

Miles tried to control his face but couldn't. His mouth formed into a wide grin.

"I'll do it," Bat said again as she walked out of the office. "I'll do it."

4.

Interview with Catherine

Q: So, a doctorate in art history at the University of Missouri, Kansas City?

A: Yes, with an emphasis in Meso-American and Native American arts.

Q: Almost done?

A: Almost. The dean has issued the certificate of acceptance of my dissertation and I'm working with the supervisory committee chair to arrange for the defense.

Q: Defense?

A: Of my dissertation.

Q: Sorry. I never went on to graduate school.

A: No worries. It's a different world.

Q: So, basically you're almost done.

A: Yes! Knock on wood. Six years of my life.

Q: Six years? My goodness. I wouldn't have the patience.

A: But I'm almost done and finally ready to find a real job.

Q: California?

A: (*Laughs.*) Ah, your sneaky way to ask about Miles.

Q: Well, yes. If you don't mind.

A: No, not all. He's a sweetheart. Coming out soon to see me.

Q: In the flesh.

A: Yes, in the flesh. I don't know how people dated before the Internet.

Q: (*Laughs.*)

A: What?

Q: You make me feel like a dinosaur.

A: Why?

Q: I met my husband in college, before the Internet. We were both English majors. Met in a seminar on Blake.

A: Oh! You look great for your age!

Q: Thanks, I think. Anyway, tell me about Miles.

A: Underemployed. He's so incredibly intelligent. He just needs to get back on track. Graduate school. That's where he should be.

Q: Are you nervous about seeing him?

A: Of course! But this really feels right. We'll have some time to get to know each other. And we'll finally have real sex.

Q: A lot of pressure.

A: No, it's going to be fun.

Q: What about defending your dissertation?

A: He'll be back on the plane to L.A. just when I need to focus. Not to worry.

Q: And so your job search will include L.A.?

A: What?

Q: Don't you want to end up in L.A. with Miles?

A: I'd rather die than live in L.A. My ideal job would be with a museum in New Mexico or maybe Arizona. But I know I'll probably have to teach for a while at a college to build up my résumé.

Q: Does Miles know that? You know, about you hating L.A.?

A: Of course! That's what I love about him. We can talk and talk and talk.

Q: But I think he wants to convince you to expand your job search to include Southern California.

A: I know. It'll be tough sledding for him, at least for a bit. But I'll convince him. L.A. hasn't been that kind to him, right? He needs to expand his horizons. If not, his own personal civilization will go into decline.

Q: What?

A: You know that the Maya population centers of the southern lowlands went into decline during the eighth and ninth centuries and were eventually abandoned altogether? There's no universally accepted theory to explain this. Some say it was precipitated by civil war, or perhaps an invasion by another people. Even overpopulation has been posited as a reason. Climate change, disease, overhunting. A lot of theories. But you know what I think?

Q: This sounds like a defense of your dissertation.

A: (*Laughs.*) Yes, it does. So, what I theorize is that the Maya failed to adapt, as a people, to whatever changes came upon them. It was almost as if they collectively forgot how to adjust to change regardless of the cause.

Q: And how does this relate to Miles?

A: If he doesn't see that L.A. is killing him—sucking the life
out of his dreams—if he doesn't do something about that,
then he will enter a decline, if he hasn't already.

Q: Harsh.

A: But true.

Q: And what happens if you can't convince him to follow you
to wherever you land a job? Do you think he'd relocate to
New Mexico or Arizona or wherever?

A: If I were a betting woman, yes. But I'm not a betting woman.

5.

Ventura Boulevard runs east–west beginning at Valley Circle Boulevard,
across seventeen concrete and asphalt miles through Woodland Hills,
Tarzana, Encino, Sherman Oaks, and ending in Studio City where it
transmutes magically into Cahuenga Boulevard, which snakes its way
through the pass into Hollywood. David remembered what the nuns
had taught him about the San Fernando Valley's history, where Ventura
Boulevard had played a starring role because it had been part of the
legendary Camino Real, the well-trodden trail connecting the Spanish
missions in the late 1700s and early 1800s, religious outposts established
by the Franciscan order to spread Roman Catholicism to the native
people. Now you could buy virtually anything on Ventura Boulevard,
from pet supplies to fat deli sandwiches, medical marijuana to imported
granite, soccer shoes to garden supplies. Oh, those Franciscans would just
shit if they were here today to see what their holy trail had wrought! David
eased his BMW into a spot just past Le Frite Café. He waited for the traffic
to clear up before hopping out of his car and then slid his Visa card into the
meter. He knew this was stupid, but David wanted to see if he could find
Bat in her work environment. Before she ran off, she'd said that there was a
bus stop on the corner that would take her to her job. Just a few blocks on
Ventura, she had explained.

David had misjudged where that coffee house was. He thought it was
on the same block as Le Frite, but apparently not. His manager Nate had
always driven them there, the few blocks from the Woodland Hills store,
and so the coffee house's precise location never fully imprinted itself on
David's memory. He walked east on Ventura, searching the signs on the
storefronts. Aha! That's it! Lot 49! What a stupid name. He jogged a bit

but then stopped, slowed down, tried to be cool. His heart started to beat in his throat. What the hell was happening? ¡Pendejo! She's just another woman. That's all. Just another night of sex.

David entered Lot 49 and let his eyes adjust. The espresso machines hissed, the calming aroma of coffee filled his lungs. Unseen speakers softly emitted a Beatles song. David looked around the room. Ah, there she was. Bat chatted with an elderly gentleman as she handed him a steaming mug emblazoned with a golden trumpet above the words *Lot 49*. The old man smiled, clearly enchanted by this kind, radiant young woman. The man dropped a coin into the tip jar, nodded, and walked to a table that was directly in front of where David stood. Bat's eyes widened, as did her smile, and she offered a little wave to the man she had been with all night.

David realized at that moment that this little affair was going to be different from all the rest. How, he didn't know. He took a step forward and stopped. Yes, he thought, this is going to be different from all the rest.

Nate Klayman's parents never fully understood their son's decision to accept David Rey's offer to manage the Woodland Hills lighting fixture store. But ultimately, they figured it wasn't the end of the world. Nate would make some money, learn how to be on his own, get it out of his system, maybe tamp down that desire *not* to be a lawyer just like his father, or a trial court judge like his mother. Almost all of their friends were suffering through the same phase: children who didn't want to follow in their parents' footsteps or at least make more logical, practical career decisions. But Ben Klayman and Ruth Rosten-Klayman knew from the moment he could talk that Nate, their only child, did things his way. His first full sentence: "I do it!" Stubborn, smart, a hell of an athlete, Nate Klayman followed his heart, listened to himself, as he played soccer first in the Maccabi League and then at El Camino Real High School, majored in English literature at Stanford, and then went on to the Anderson School of Management at UCLA. He could have earned his law degree as well, but he liked the idea of becoming a literate businessman who left the legal intricacies to, well, lawyers.

But why wasn't he a young executive at a major corporation? What was so enticing about working at a chain of lighting fixture stores for a man who never finished college (but who obviously had an innate talent for business) while their friends' children made less exotic professional choices? Was there something Hemingwayesque about it? That's what Ruth thought . . . working for a man of the people—a handsome, charismatic man, a man who came from very little, who made quite an impression in the commercials that blanketed the late night hours on cable and radio spots on AM talk and news stations. All very adventurous and literary. Well, at least Nate worked within walking distance of his parents' lovingly kept two-story home south of Ventura Boulevard, and but a mile from Temple Aliyah on Valley Circle where he became a bar mitzvah at age thirteen. He was a good boy even if they didn't fully understand his life decisions.

Next issue: Nate needed to get more serious about his girlfriend, Adina, or else he was going to lose her. They'd known each other in high school and temple, both got into Stanford where they finally started dating their junior year (she majored in political science . . . smart move), and should have been engaged long ago, right? The families had known each other for years, and Nate's parents had secretly hoped—ever since Nate and Adina were teenagers—that a romance would bloom and lead to marriage someday. Their minds had filled with dreams of success and beautiful grandchildren when Nate and Adina walked hand-in-hand before and after the Stanford graduation ceremony. And now that both were back home, Adina landing an exciting job being the field representative for their congresswoman where she handled local policy issues and served as the principal liaison between the congressional office and neighborhood businesses, organizations, and citizens. And *she* was thinking about applying to law school! At least that's what Ben had heard at the temple Men's Club meeting two weeks ago. Adina's father, Eli, was bragging a bit, and he had a tendency to exaggerate, so who knows. But the point remained the same: Adina was moving on with her life. Beautiful, smart, practical Adina. Nate better get moving with his.

As Nate walked through the Woodland Hills store just before opening, chatting with his sales team, sipping a fresh cup of French roast in his favorite (slightly cracked) Stanford mug, he knew nothing of his parents' angst. In fact, as far as he could tell, they had backed each of his decisions without a hint of hesitation or concern. And that's because Ben and Ruth loved their only son with all their hearts, with their entire beings. He was their gift from God. Ruth had gone through six miscarriages before she carried a baby to term. Ruth was a stubborn woman (so she wasn't too surprised that Nate had inherited that trait) and she would not give up on having her own baby. So when Nate told them that he wanted to major in English during winter break of his sophomore year, Ruth had exclaimed: "Wonderful!" Ben let out: "You were always a big reader!" In fact, after their initial, elated reactions, the rest of the conversation went like this:

BEN: So, English, huh?

NATE: Yes! They have an amazing department!

RUTH: Honey, of course they do. It's one of the top universities in the country.

BEN: In the world, actually.

RUTH: Yes, in the world! I'm sure every department is top notch.

BEN: We're very proud of you, Nate.

NATE: Thank you.

RUTH: And you know we love you to pieces.

BEN: Yes, we do.

NATE: I love you guys, too.

And that same night, as Nate met up with friends from his old high school class, Ben and Ruth huddled on their living room couch wondering what Nate would ever be able to do with a degree in English. Teach? But he'd need to get a master's and then a PhD if he wanted to be a college professor. And there were so few jobs in academia, at least if you wanted to stay in Los Angeles. The market was flooded with gifted and brilliant graduates of the best schools all scrambling for the same limited slots. And most of the openings were non-tenure-track, part-time "lecturer" positions without health insurance, let alone job security. Highly educated slaves. They'd both read that in a *New Republic* article just two months ago. Maybe law school was still on the table. In fact, Ben said that one of the best young associates at his firm had double-majored at USC in English and economics, then went on to law school at Yale, for goodness sake! Yep, that young woman (Debra Lee, that was her name) could write a damn good brief, in plain English, no legalese. And her first language was Korean! She understood the business side of being a lawyer, too. Definitely partnership material. So it all could work out once Nate's little lark was out of his system. Okay, Ben and Ruth agreed, no more worries.

He'll be fine. But each continued to lose sleep in secret thinking that the other had moved on.

Nate loved Saturday mornings at the store. Inevitably, Adina would spend the night, so when he woke at six, without the help of an alarm clock, he'd slip out of bed, get into workout clothes, and go for a run. By the time he got back she'd be awake at the kitchen table, clutching a cup of coffee, looking slightly rumpled in one of Nate's T-shirts, beautiful with a sleepy smile. Oh, that smile! That smile made him fall for her back in college despite years of denying any attraction. This was the woman he wanted to marry, to have children with. But Adina wasn't ready just yet. No rush, she always said whenever he broached the subject. We're still young. Why not live together? No, no, she said. Her father would just die. Besides, they lived close to each other so why rock the boat? In the end, Nate had to accept his circumstances and was content to have Adina stay over Friday and Saturday nights, making his weekend mornings blessed.

And this morning followed his usual weekend pattern. After a hot shower and downing a Zone cashew pretzel bar with a large glass of water, Nate filled his thermos with coffee, accepted a delicious, deep kiss from Adina, and drove his seven-year-old Subaru Outback to the store. Very little could improve his life as far as he was concerned. He loved Adina, he loved his job, and he was healthy. What more could a person want?

As this particular Saturday began, Nate strode to and fro, Stanford mug in hand, talking to his sales team before the store opened and customers wandered in looking for that perfect lamp for the den or pondering track lighting for a son or daughter. There he was, learning a *real* business that welcomed *real* customers with *real* and practical needs. Not major finance. Not Apple or Exxon Mobil or General Electric or Archer Daniels Midland, but a healthy, thirteen-store chain that sold lighting fixtures to parents and young adults and senior citizens. Bringing light to the world! Ain't nothin' wrong with that.

Nate heard a rap on the plate glass door and turned away from Michele, his assistant sales manager, who had been explaining that a storm back east had delayed a shipment of Possini plug-in swing-arm wall lamps. There stood David Rey holding a paper cup of Lot 49 coffee in his right hand, his left frozen in place after knocking on the glass. Nate told Michele to hang on, the boss was here, and went to let David into the store.

"Sorry, forgot my key," said David as he entered.

Nate stood back to let David pass. He couldn't remember the last time his boss apologized for anything.

"No problem," said Nate.

The two men stood facing one another, each holding their coffee, the elder three inches taller than the younger. Nate looked into David's eyes and saw something in them he'd never seen before. Fear. Embarrassment. Giddiness. All mixed together.

"Let's look at the inventory," David finally said.

"It's under control."

David frowned. "I want to look at the inventory. With you."

Nate smiled, nodded, knew that David wanted to talk in private. Checking inventory was David's way of avoiding a tough issue like firing one of his managers or relocating a store. When they entered the large back room that held a menagerie of lighting fixtures, lampshades, and bulbs, not to mention various accouterments of the home—end tables, mirrors, decorative knick-knacks, gewgaws, and tchotchkes—David asked a lone employee with a clipboard and Sharpie to please leave for a few minutes and close the door behind him, thanks. Nate suddenly felt sick. This was serious. What was wrong? Had Nate screwed something up really badly? Was someone stealing from the store, maybe emptying a bank account during the night? David looked about the room, examined the well-stocked shelves, his mind clearly roiling with something. Nate wanted to ask what was up, but he knew better.

"How is your girlfriend?" David finally asked before taking a self-conscience sip from his coffee.

"Adina?"

"You have another girlfriend I don't know about?" David smiled. "Yes, Adina. How is she?"

It was Nate's turn to take a sip of coffee. What should he say?

"I hope she's well," said David.

"Oh, yes," Nate said and then coughed. "She's great. We're great."

"That's great."

Nate glanced at the large clock that hung on the far wall, just above David's head. David turned around and snorted.

"Not to worry, Nate, the store will open just fine without you."

"Yes, right . . ."

David sighed. "Sorry, Nate."

"No, it's okay."

"Something's happened, that's all."

Nate caught his breath. "Everything okay? You're okay?"

"Fuck."

Every possible nightmare scenario paraded through Nate's mind. David was bankrupt. David was dying. David was . . . who knows? Nate felt as if he couldn't breathe.

"I met a girl," said David as he stared at his coffee cup. "I mean, a young woman. Last night. We spent the night together."

Nate's entire body relaxed. David normally did not share much about his dating life other than to brag just a bit every so often. This was different. Nate finally asked: "That's a good thing, right?"

David shook his head, not in disagreement but in confusion.

"What's wrong with her?"

David stifled a laugh. "Wrong? Nothing. She's perfect."

"Nobody's perfect."

David nodded. "Perfect to me."

Nate offered a big grin. "That's fantastic!"

David searched for a trash can. When he found one right behind his left leg, he let his half-full coffee cup fall into it. The Lot 49 cup made a louder sound than either David or Nate expected. A small geyser of coffee shot up from the small hole at the top of the plastic lid and splashed onto David's gray wool slacks.

"Shit," he muttered as bent down to wipe away the coffee from his left pant leg. "Is it fantastic that I can't stop thinking of her?"

"It's only been one night."

"That's the problem," said David as he straightened up and locked onto Nate's eyes. "I want more than one night."

Nate sipped his coffee not knowing what to say.

David continued: "I tracked her down this morning, to Lot 49, just to see her face again. We have plans for tonight. Dinner."

"Haven't you felt this way before?"

"Of course. With my first wife. And that didn't end well."

Nate finally understood. "A great man said: 'The one good thing about repeating your mistakes is that you know when to cringe.'"

David's face softened. He smiled. "Sounds like a dicho."

"A what?"

"A Mexican saying."

Nate thought about it. Then said: "I think Solzhenitsyn said it. Definitely not Mexican."

"Russian?"

"Definitely Russian."

"Well," said David, "Russians can be as wise as Mexicans . . . sometimes."

Both men jumped just a bit as a clerk pushed the door open and marched straight to a shelf at the back wall, squinted at the boxes of bulbs, then quickly grabbed what she had been searching for. When she left, Nate looked up at the wall clock again.

"Go," said David. "Your customers await you."

6.

Interview with Adina

Q: Looking forward to anything?

A: Third season of *Downton Abbey*. Sixty-six days and counting.

Q: Anything else?

A: Oh, Obama's second term.

Q: You think there'll be one?

A: It's in the bag. I'd trust Nate Silver with my life.

Q: Speaking of men named Nate, what about you and your Nate?

A: Oh, we're great.

Q: What's next for you two?

A: I don't know. What do you have in mind?

Q: Marriage?

A: Definitely not.

Q: Really? But, he's head over heels for you.

A: And he makes me so happy, too. But that doesn't mean marriage, does it? What about my plans?

Q: What kind of plans?

A: I kicked butt at Stanford. Phi Beta Kappa. My résumé is filled with things most people would kill for. I want to go to Harvard or Yale for law school. And then D.C. That's where I want to settle. How does Nate fit in *that* picture? I would never ask him to follow me across the country, get some shit job for three years while I'm getting my law degree, and then sniff after my heels like a dog when I move to D.C. for a job with the federal government. That wouldn't be fair, would it? He's made a nice life out here for himself. He loves his parents and likes spending time with them. I don't want to be responsible for messing up all that.

Q: I'm sure he thinks you two will marry.

A: I think deep down he knows I'm not staying around forever. That we're not going to grow old together.

Q: You haven't discussed it yet? You know . . . your plans?

A: The time will come. It always does.

7.

"When were you going to tell me?" said David in a low sputter.

Bat turned to look at the couple two tables over. They appeared to be not more than three or four years older than she, probably just started their first real jobs, falling in love during a company holiday party or softball game. Nice and uncomplicated. Not like her life. When Bat was a little girl, she sometimes wished that she could be her black cat, Sooty, who slept most of the day away on the sun-warmed rug in the living room. No worries beyond being comfortable. Bat turned away from the couple and focused on her food, a plate filled with a beautiful piece of grilled salmon, crisp broccoli, a steaming baked potato. Untouched. She finally looked up.

"We're not married, you know."

David blinked. "You and me?"

"No," she said with a shake of her head. "Me and Uri. Yes, we're dating, but we don't live together. And I'm sure he's gone out on me."

"Oh, so this—you and me—was a revenge thing?"

"No, of course not."

Bat reached for her fork and then picked slowly at the salmon.

"So, it's simple," said David. "You can break up with him as easily as you jumped into bed with me."

That was it. Bat stood and threw her fork onto the tabletop. It caromed off the side of her plate with a loud *CLACK!* and then bounced once onto the carpeted floor. Most of the Red Lobster patrons looked up from their meals and conversations. A waiter made a move as if to intervene but then froze to see what was going to happen next.

"Fuck you," she whispered.

Fallbrook Avenue was humming with traffic as Bat made her way toward the bus stop. She had purposely chosen a restaurant in the West Valley just in case this kind of scene happened. David had complained about her choice of the Red Lobster, but she prevailed. Now her stomach lurched and growled and she castigated herself for not waiting until after dinner, after they went back to his place for one last night in bed, to tell David of Uri's existence. Stupid, stupid, stupid. Now, she'd get home and heat up a Healthy Choice frozen dinner and drink half a bottle of wine in her little kitchen.

When Bat sat at the bus stop, she pulled out her phone to check her e-mail and text messages. Two texts from Uri. One saying that he couldn't wait to get home at the end of the week. And the other saying that he loved her. Shit. Bat had lied to David about Uri probably cheating on her. She had no reason to think that, no evidence whatsoever. But she needed to rationalize herself to David, to prove she was not an asshole.

"This is silly."

Bat looked up. David stood in front of her holding two to-go containers.

"Yes, it is," she said.

"Let's go to my house," said David. "We can salvage our evening."

"And?"

David coughed, looked around and then back down to Bat's expectant face. He smiled.

Bat returned the smile.

"The food should heat up pretty well, right?" she said without moving from the bench.

"Yes," said David extending his free hand to Bat. "It will all be fine."

And so they worked out a truce, an understanding. They would enjoy themselves until Uri came back from Israel, then they would stop, cold turkey, no more affair. Nada más. She didn't want to know anything about David's life, and David couldn't inquire into hers. Actually, Bat was the one who came up with the proposal, and David had little choice but to accept. She had asked him three times: Can you live with this deal? *Deal?* he had asked, a little surprised by how cold the word sounded. Yes, she'd responded. Deal. Can you live with it? Yes, he'd said. I must.

8.

Interview with Uri

Q: Finally, a man.

A: Excuse me?

Q: Sorry. He's had me interview only women so far. I was wondering if he was trying to make some kind of point.

A: Who's he?

Q: Olivas.

A: Actually, he's quite nice. Very polite. But much shorter than I expected.

Q: You've met him? In the flesh?

A: Well, yes. You haven't?

Q: No. He insists on e-mail and phone calls. He says he's too busy for meetings.

A: We had a very nice lunch, actually. Downtown where he works.

Q: I'm getting jealous.

A: (*Laughs.*) No need for jealousy. It just turns out we have a lot in common. His wife has relatives in Tel Aviv, where I was born. My parents still live there.

Q: So, you just got back from visiting them?

A: Yes. Oh, it was so wonderful. I think of moving back there sometime. But I doubt Bat would do that. She's busy with school and Lot 49. Plus her family is here, too. And I'm starting a new job next week, anyway.

Q: Oh? Where?

A: Rey's Lighting Fixtures in Encino.

Q: Really?

A: I'm replacing the last manager, who's moving back up to San Francisco with her boyfriend. Elise. Nice person. But she has a chance to begin a new life. Who can blame her? Anyway, she's training me and then off she goes.

Q: What does Bat think of your new job?

A: She's funny that way. I tried to tell her about it but she just wanted to know that I had a job and that I was happy about it. She didn't want to know what kind of job it was.

Q: Maybe you should tell her.

A: But why does it matter? She's fine not knowing, at least for now. Eventually she'll have some reason to visit me at work and then she'll need to find out.

Q: I suppose so, though she seems oddly disconnected from you.

A: You don't know Bat. She operates differently than you and I.

Q: You could say that.

A: (*Laughs.*) I just did.

9.

"Is Uri a common name?"

Nate looked up from his desk. "Yes, I guess."

David stood in the middle of Nate's office. He clutched the employment application of Uri Har-Paz.

"So, there are a lot of Uris running around the Valley, you think?"

Nate stared at David wondering where this was going. He nodded.

"What does 'Har-Paz' mean?"

Nate closed his laptop and sat back in his chair. "Well, that's actually kind of interesting."

"Is it?"

"Yes," Nate said with a little chuckle. "It literally means 'Goldberg.'"

David took a seat in the chair in front of Nate's desk and got ready for one of Nate's famous Jewish history lessons.

"So, after World War II, when Jews could return to the new state of Israel, there was this movement for the Hebraization of surnames."

David knew that this was where he asked: "Which means?"

"Basically, immigrants to Israel translated their surnames to Hebrew to remove the remnants of being an exiled people. Because, you see, a lot of Jews in places like Germany were forced to take non-Jewish names. Kind of like a slave name, you know, with African Americans." Nate crossed his arms. "And it's still happening today. Many of the thousands of Israelis who apply for legal name changes each year do it to adopt Hebrew names."

David nodded. He understood.

"So a last name like Weingarten became Kerem, which means 'vineyard' in Hebrew. Lerner became Lamdan. And Goldberg was changed to Har-Paz."

"Ah. Uri Har-Paz would have been Uri Goldberg if his grandparents hadn't changed it."

"Right. Pretty interesting stuff, isn't it?"

"Tell me," said David. "When did I hire Mr. Uri Har-Paz to manage my Encino store?"

Nate reopened his laptop and tapped a few keys.

"You gave the okay last month, Tuesday the fifteenth to be exact."

"Really?"

"E-mails don't lie," said Nate. "At least, not usually. You really don't remember?"

"No."

"You said that you were too busy and that you trusted me to make the final decision."

"Well, his application looks good. I see why I approved your recommendation."

"Hire hard, supervise easy, a great man once told me."

"Who was that?"

Nate laughed. "You did, boss. You did."

"I have no doubt he'll work out just fine."

"Yes," said Nate. "You'll like Uri. He's a straight shooter. And he has a very cute girlfriend. I'm sure you'd approve."

David tried not to react. "You've met his girlfriend?"

"Yes, a few times, actually. She works at Lot 49. You might have seen her, too."

David stood. "I'll pay the Encino store a visit this weekend."

"Want me to join you?"

"No need, I can introduce myself without help," said David as he walked away from the desk and toward the showroom. "It's important for me to keep up with my managers."

David made several visits to the Encino store, meeting with Uri, checking the sales figures, spending time with the staff. He came to this conclusion: Uri was a good man. He was smart, hardworking, loyal. He had a way with the customers, and the staff respected him. Nate had made a good choice. Hire hard, supervise easy.

But as the weeks passed, David's desire to be with Bat grew stronger, less susceptible to willpower. And as he spoke with Uri about inventory and customer service and payroll, David couldn't stop his imagination from taking him to unpleasant places . . . places where Uri touched Bat's naked body, kissed her plump lips, put himself into her. As Uri's mouth moved and said things having to do with lighting fixtures, David could hear Bat moan and moan and moan until she came. No! This was too much! David had to do something. But what? He had to see Bat again and then he'd—they'd—figure out what to do.

But wait. Think, think . . .

David needed to talk to Nate. Before going to Bat. Before doing something very, very stupid. So one Thursday at the end of the workday, David invited Nate out for a drink. Nate happily accepted, particularly since Adina was in D.C. with her congresswoman to get ready for yet another hearing on Benghazi. The Democrats on the committee had to counteract the Republican witch hunt. When Nate suggested TGI Fridays, David said no, he wanted something a little different . . . what about BJ's not far from there? They "handcrafted" beer right on the premises. Yes! That sounded great.

And there they sat in a booth across from each other, the elder caressing a glass of Harvest Hefeweizen, the younger sipping a Tatonka Stout, plates of crispy fried artichokes and spinach-stuffed mushrooms between them. But it took a full beer before David could share his secret with Nate. So, on their second glass, David leaned forward, elbows on the tabletop, fingertips softly tapping the cold, perspiring glass of beer. And he told Nate everything about Bat and Uri, slowly at first, then speeding up once he knew there was no turning back. Nate listened carefully, stoically withholding comment until his boss finished his tale. When David was done, he sat back, spent. He lifted his tired eyes up to Nate, and waited. Nate blinked, let out a loud breath, then took a sip of beer. His mouth opened slightly, ready to say something, offer advice or comment of some sort. Then his mouth closed slowly. Nate furrowed his brow.

"Walk away," he finally said.

"What?" said David, looking as if Nate had slapped him.

"This is a lawsuit waiting to happen."

"What do you mean?" said David as he sat straight in his seat. "We're talking about a woman, not a car crash."

"It might as well be a car crash if you fire Uri."

"Who said fire? I never said that."

"Let's think this through," said Nate. "If you somehow get between Uri and Bat—and based on everything Uri tells me, they're doing just fine in the romance department—how could you keep Uri on? That would give a new meaning to the word *awkward.*"

"I can deal with awkward as long as I have Bat."

"But could Uri?"

"So if he can't deal with it, he can quit."

Nate sighed. "In business school, we learned about this thing called 'constructive discharge.' It basically means that you've made things so uncomfortable for an employee, he quits. Then he can turn around and sue you. And that wouldn't look very nice in the *Times*, would it? Headline: THE KING OF LIGHTING FIXTURES SUED IN LOVE TRIANGLE. Not good."

David knew Nate was right.

"Is she really that special?"

David nodded. He looked like a little boy whose favorite toy had been stolen.

"Is there another way?" asked David. "Could I offer Uri something?"

"You mean, buy Bat from him?"

"No!" said David. "And just because we're having beer and talking about personal things, don't forget who pays your very nice salary."

Nate's mouth snapped shut. He turned away. David knew he'd gone too far.

"I shouldn't have said that."

Nate took a sip of beer. "Don't worry about it."

They sat without speaking for almost two minutes.

"What if I offer him a manager's position in one of my other stores," said David with a little smile. "You know, up in Sacramento."

"Why would he move up there?"

"I could offer him a big fat bonus on top of his current salary."

Nate shook his head. "Why the hell would you do that? That doesn't make sense!"

"Sure it does," said David. "I could say that he's doing such a great job in Encino, we could really use his talents in Sacramento, where a person with his qualifications is harder to find."

"And what if he accepts and Bat follows him up there?"

"She won't," said David as he held his palms toward his young, inexperienced employee.

"Why not?"

"She's at a top university and her family is here."

"So?"

"So you apparently don't know how Mexicans think."

Nate's lips started to move into place, ready to respond, but then his mouth froze and he remained silent.

"Don't worry," said David as he returned his hands to the glass of beer. "It will all work out."

"If you say so," said Nate. "You're always right."

"Not always," laughed David. "Only when I really want something."

10.

Interview with Bat

Q: How are you holding up?

A: What do you mean?

Q: You know, with Uri breaking up with you and moving to Sacramento?

A: Oh, well, he's been gone almost three months now. And here I am, still alive.

Q: Of course. I wasn't implying that he was the be-all-and-end-all.

A: No offense taken. I understand what you're getting at. It was kind of obvious that I sometimes saw him as the man I'd eventually make a life with . . . have children with, make a home together. That scared me. I've always been independent. I guess that's why I had that fling with David. I needed to prove something to myself. But when I realized that I was going to throw away a good thing, I imposed the moratorium on the cheating. But I guess the irony gods had their laugh. Turns out Uri needed to prove himself as a professional more than he needed me.

Q: That's very big of you, considering.

A: Considering what?

Q: The circumstances.

A: (*Rubs tummy.*) You mean this?

Q: That's part of it. When are you due?

A: Five more months. (*Grins.*) The timing will work out. I'll take some time off from school. Already worked it out with UCLA. They're very supportive. I'm not the first undergraduate to get pregnant.

Q: What about Lot 49? Miles?

A: Oh, Miles has been so wonderful. He's not mad, he understands. And the thing with Catherine didn't go anywhere, so he's back full time. Everyone's been very supportive.

Q: It's great that you're being so positive about this.

A: Oh, don't get me wrong. I totally freaked out after the third pregnancy test confirmed what the first two had. But when I made the decision to keep it, I found peace. As my mother says: Donde una puerta se cierra, otra se abre.

Q: Is David a door that opened and Uri the one that closed?

A: I was wondering when you were going to ask. He's been great ever since Uri left. He let me cry and all the stuff most men hate seeing. He acts tough, at least in business, but he's all marshmallow inside.

Q: Don't you think it's odd that Uri works for David?

A: Actually, when I finally put two and two together and told David that his Uri was also my Uri—this was after Uri told me he was moving to Sacramento—we both laughed. I mean, it was so fucking weird. David kept saying that he couldn't believe it, that he hadn't realized it until I told him.

Q: That's what he said? He couldn't believe it?

A: Yep.

Q: Interesting.

A: Life is full of coincidences. One time I was in line at Target and I started talking to this guy in front of me. One thing led to another . . . you know how random conversations go . . . and we eventually figured out that he was the brother of my cousin Alma's landlord. How weird is that?

Q: But this is a stranger coincidence, don't you think?

A: Well, maybe. Six degrees of separation, right?

Q: It's more like two degrees. And now you're back with David since Uri is out of the picture.

A: Well, when you put it that way, it all sounds kind of like a Dickens novel.

Q: So?

A: David and I never really talked about Uri, except that David said good things about him and his value to the company and all that. And when he asked for a transfer to the Sacramento store, David said that he didn't want to lose him so he okayed it.

Q: That's what David said?

A: Yes. Why are you acting so weird?

Q: No, sorry. I'm out of line. Forgive me.

A: Sure.

Q: Tell me about the baby.

A: (*Smiles.*) Well, at first I thought it was the end of the world. I'm pro-choice and all, but for me, personally, I just couldn't wrap my head around it—you know, getting an abortion.

Q: And what does David think?

A: Oh, he's been wonderful.

Q: Is it his?

A: You don't fuck around, do you?

Q: Sorry, again. But I think that's a question our readers would want asked, don't you?

A: Yep. You're right. I'm not certain if it's his. Deep down, I think it is. But David said that he'd be a good papá regardless of the truth. He said that if Uri found out about it, we could say David was the father. Like I said, he's been great. He's helping with the finances. And we're sort of dating, if you can call it that. Very low key. We're a thing, I guess.

Q: Do you feel odd about that?

A: I did at first, yes. But you know, it's not about me at this point. And besides, I think I love David.

Q: Really?

A: Yes. I know he's older than I am, but he's tender and he always tells me what's on his mind. That kind of honesty is hard to find in a man, don't you think?

Q: (*Coughs.*) Yes, of course. You're a lucky girl.

A: Yes, I am. The luckiest. Oh, wait, listen . . .

Q: What?

A: This song. I love it. It's by the Brazilian Girls. My new favorite group.

Q: I like it. Are they new?

A: Nah. They've been around for about seven or eight years, but they never were on my radar until recently. It's kind of funny because they blend electronica with chanson, house, tango, reggae, lounge. But no Brazilian rhythms at all. And no one is from Brazil. *And* there's only one female in the group.

Q: Lie upon lie.

A: (*Laughs.*) It's art. Art doesn't lie.

Q: Oh, one more thing. Why do people call you Bat? Why not Birdie if you don't like Bertha? That would make more sense, wouldn't it?

A: You know, there was this nice older gentleman who used to come into Lot 49. His name was Herman. He passed away last year. Anyway, he had tattooed numbers on his right forearm that peeked out from his long-sleeve shirt when he paid me. He always wore long sleeves even when it was the middle of summer. Anyway, I knew what the numbers were.

Q: Holocaust survivor?

A: Yes, and I asked him about it. He didn't want to say too much about it. Herman had the sweetest smile. He's the one who first called me Bat.

Q: Why?

A: He said it meant "daughter." Pretty special, right?

Q: Yes. Pretty special. Want another herbal tea?

A: Sure, why not. If you're buying.

Q: Of course. My treat.

A: You're the best.

Q: Thanks. It's nice to hear it every so often.

Pluck

I step into the bathtub, and Mamá stands in the doorway telling me to be careful, don't slip and crack your head.

As I ease myself into the hot water, she says: Mija, what is that?

I freeze, my butt just touching the water's surface. What's what? I ask.

She says: You got hair now? Down there? She covers her mouth when she says this, like she's about to throw up.

I never told her that I got my first period last month. My older sister Celia told me to keep it secret from Mamá. I asked her why but she just shook her head, face all screwed up like she ate something bad.

Mamá walks to the sink, opens a drawer, and pulls out tweezers. She holds them up, squints like she's trying to see if they're okay. Then she looks at me.

Get out, she says. Get out now.

Still Life with Woman and Stroller

You see her each morning at seven, almost precisely the time you're having your first cup of coffee, sitting at the Dell laptop you've set up on your grandmother's old rosewood desk that you've stationed in front of the bay window so you can feel as if you're enjoying the beautiful Los Angeles weather while you're really just starting a day of procrastination when you should be working on your freelance writing and getting more paying gigs so you don't lose this little two-bedroom, one-bath house that is your palace despite the recent leaving of your boyfriend who moved out three weeks ago this Tuesday.

And this woman pushes a very expensive Orbit baby stroller while the French roast coffee warms your face as you sip from the large KCRW coffee mug that was a premium for that thirty-five-dollar donation you made but really couldn't afford but you figured it was a good public radio investment for when you fulfill your real passion, completing that half-finished novel about a Chicana who is the first in her family to go to college and has written for some of the best online publications such as *Salon* and the *Huffington Post* and the *Los Angeles Review of Books* and *The Rumpus* but who finally finds an agent and publishes her novel with Random House and then *Bookworm*'s Michael Silverblatt discovers this "lyrical new voice" and the rest is history, as they say. And it would be rather embarrassing when the real Michael Silverblatt learns that this young novelist listens to KCRW but never gave money, even during the pledge drive, so why should he give her the time of day when she can't even pay for the enjoyment public radio gives her? Money well spent, no doubt. Plus the mug is nice.

The woman stops right in front of your house—something she never does—pulls out her iPhone, and swipes the screen a few times. And then you see it. You realize it's not a baby. You squint, try to focus on its little head. He—she—it is really strange looking. Strange *is* the word for it. It's very small and gray, except for a white stripe down the center of its face. It meows but you can't hear it through your too-expensive double-paned bay window. But it clearly is meowing and blinking and then licking its little furry lips. The woman reaches down and scratches the cat's neck, which the cat clearly loves.

The woman pats the cat's head for good measure, puts her iPhone into the back pocket of her jeans that are too tight—if anyone asked you— jeans that show off every curve of her round ass that most men would die for, leave their girlfriends for, just like your boyfriend, Mario, who, in fact, left you for this woman with the tight jeans and the cat in the stroller. And you watch as she restarts her journey, pushing the stroller along this Los Angeles street on this beautiful Los Angeles morning, the precise morning that you promise yourself that your life will begin in earnest, that your literary passions will be fulfilled, finally and without any further delay. The morning you will recount in superb detail when Michael Silverblatt interviews you at the KCRW radio station in Santa Monica that you helped support with a thirty-five-dollar donation. An auspicious Los Angeles morning when true art—and your life—bloomed.

A Very Bitter Man

Long ago, at the far end of the town, there lived a very bitter man. Some said he was born bitter. Others said he became bitter slowly, year by year, because his parents were not nice people. Regardless of the reason, the bitter man was not pleasant to be around. The people of the town left him to his own devices and they tried not to tread on the road that ran by his dilapidated house.

Being left alone was the only thing that made the bitter man happy.

How bitter was this man? Well, he was so bitter that he did not even want to share his broken-down old house with his own shadow. So, most days and nights, he kept his windows shut tight with the dusty old curtains closed so that the light of the sun or moon would not shine in and cast his shadow within the house.

But the bitter man could not hide in his house all day. Even he had to eat. Thus, each morning he would creep out of his dark and musty house to pick mangoes that hung from the big trees that shaded his house.

One such morning, as he reached for a mango, he heard his front door shut with a loud crack. In a panic, the man ran to the house.

"Who is in there?" the man bellowed as he pounded the heavy wooden door with his fist.

"Your shadow," came the response.

The bitter man's eyes widened in disbelief and fear. *Is this a trick?* he thought. He had to discover the truth.

"Prove it!" yelled the bitter man.

And what happened next was most remarkable. The voice on the other side of the door proceeded to recite many secret things that only the bitter man could know such as when the man ate each day, which side he slept on, how many naps he took, and other little details that made this usually unflappable man blush a dark brown-red. The bitter man simply could not believe his ears. But the voice had indeed proved that it was the bitter man's shadow.

"May I come in?" asked the bitter man in the meekest voice he could manage.

There was a long silence. Finally, the small voice answered: "Only if you agree to share your life with me."

The bitter man thought for a moment. *How could this be a bad thing?* he thought. *After all, my shadow has been with me since I was a baby. Maybe it is time to share this old house.*

"Yes," said the bitter man. "You may share my home with me."

The door creaked opened. The bitter man looked down and saw his long shadow stretch across the floor of his old house. After the man entered, he opened all the curtains to let in as much sunshine as possible. At that moment, the man's bitterness melted away.

When the people of the town learned of this amazing transformation they did not mind walking past the once dark house. Indeed, if they happened to see the man sitting on his porch, they would say hello. The man would wave and offer a loud and happy greeting. And if the people had looked carefully, they would have seen the man's shadow waving a hearty hello, too.

Silver Case

María kept her eyes trained on the silver cigarette case that Dr. Templeton clutched in his right hand. She studied the Byzantine design on the case's surface. At first, María believed that she saw the outline of a horrific, satanic face, but after a few moments of concentration she discerned the contours of a rose, an overblown and sensuous example of the flower. In one fluid movement Dr. Templeton popped the case open, withdrew a cigarette, snapped it shut, tapped the cigarette on the smooth back of the case, and slid the case back into his jacket for a tweedy hibernation. The doctor then snatched a wooden match from a weighted leather cup on his desk and struck it on a rough patch on the side of the cup. The flame billowed red and blue and then subsided to a flicker before he drew it near the cigarette.

Taking a deep drag, the doctor lowered his head and looked over his glasses at María. He allowed the smoke to leak from the corners of his mouth and then, as if irritated by the mechanics of smoking, blew the remaining smoke from his nostrils with all the strength of his lungs so that he looked like an angry dragon. The plumes of smoke rose and then lingered about the doctor's unruly bush of red hair that seemed to spring from his head as if trying to escape.

"What else?" asked María in English.

Dr. Templeton looked sad, fatigued. "There's nothing else, really. The cancer has gone on too long for us to do anything."

"And the time. How much did you say?"

The doctor sighed. "Six months to a year." He put his hand on María's shoulder and he was surprised that she did not shake, but stood rock still. The nurse tried not to make much noise as she went about picking up and putting away medical files in the back of the office.

María averted her eyes from Dr. Templeton's. She stared at a beautiful calendar that hung over the doctor's massive oak desk. At the top of the calendar "1943" was emblazoned in bright blue ink, with little Easter bunnies peeking from behind the numbers while colored eggs rolled about the foreground. She imagined that her son would love that calendar.

"Here," the doctor said handing a small brown bottle of pills to María. "There's nothing wrong with using these when you have to. If the pain eventually gets too great, we can talk further."

"Thank you," she whispered. "Pray for me."

Dr. Templeton blushed so that his face matched his hair. He coughed. "Yes, Mrs. Isla. Of course I'll pray for you."

María imagined the doctor's prayer rising up to heaven like cigarette smoke and she smiled. All she needed now was a dime for the streetcar.

The Last Dream of Pánfilo Velasco

After the paintings of Gronk

One Monday evening, as he walked home from his dreary job making things nobody needed, Pánfilo Velasco saw two coffins that floated just within his peripheral vision. This did not alarm him in the least. Rather, Pánfilo knew that he was weary and that sleep was just the balm he needed.

Pánfilo entered his small, empty house, bathed, and went to bed without eating dinner. Sleep enveloped him within minutes.

And so began Pánfilo Velasco's last dream. Faces from his life flickered and shimmered into view. First, he saw his beautiful mother, Hortencia, as she looked in the photograph that appeared on the front pages of all the newspapers the day a jury convicted her of murdering the Benedetti triplets who had lived two houses down. Hortencia had never looked so exquisite! She hung herself during the fifth year of her incarceration, though some say that the guards killed her out of disgust. But Pánfilo could only be enchanted by his mother's face. He smiled as he fell deeper into his dream.

Hortencia's face faded into that of Pánfilo's brutish father, Octavio, who did not understand the poetry of wine or the splendor of certain shadows that fall upon the ground during the months of September, October, and November. Oh, Octavio's loutishness was the true crime, worse than a triple murder! Pánfilo stirred and struggled with his sheet, his heart racing.

Octavio's face eventually bled into darkness. Pánfilo's heart slowed, his limbs quieted. Soon, Pánfilo's dream vision filled with the countenance of his first lover, who went by the title "Countess" though her real name was María de la Cruz. She was the most famous prostitute who plied her trade within the town of Pánfilo's childhood. In her prime the Countess taught many a young man the ways of love, for a reasonable price. Pánfilo's loins grew warm and he let out a low moan.

Suddenly, the amorphous surroundings transformed into a beach. Pánfilo found himself standing at the edge of the water. He looked down and saw that he carried his mother's draped body. The Countess, perched upon a gigantic heart, commanded the frightened Pánfilo to step into a small boat that floated in the water before him. "What shall I do with my mother's body?" he asked. "Toss her into the boat, mi amor," she answered. And Pánfilo did what he was told. He settled in near his mother's body, and the boat started to move forward of its own volition.

As the boat steadily moved across what appeared to be an endless lake, Pánfilo forgot about his mother's body at his feet. His stomach rumbled and he allowed his mind to drift to wonderful memories of delicacies he had enjoyed throughout his life. Pánfilo remembered so many delightful foods: toast with melted cheese and roasted red chiles . . . slices of New York pizza . . . sweet blocks of candy that resembled prehistoric amber . . . salted pecans . . . charred marshmallows . . . succulent bits of ham and lamb.

The boat finally reached the other side of the lake. Pánfilo lifted his mother's body and put it upon his back. He stepped out of the boat onto the warm sand. Pánfilo grew angry with himself because he had forgotten to ask the Countess for further direction. But no matter. He would trudge forward. As he did, Pánfilo noticed that the terrain changed. He saw objects that reminded him of a mobile that hung over his bed when he was a child. And Pánfilo's burden grew heavier, as if someone had dropped a large bag of uncooked rice onto his mother's body.

After marching across the sand for a very long time, Pánfilo realized that the terrain had grown more fantastical with each step. Indeed, the shapes he saw seemed to become something more than terrain, something akin to a language. No, wait! Not merely a language . . . a hieroglyph, ancient and mysterious, that spoke only to him. Without much effort he deciphered the message. Pánfilo now knew what he needed to do.

Armed with knowledge, Pánfilo finally reached the place where he could allow his mother to rest. He looked up and saw a large boulder shaped like a hand holding a ripe fig. The boulder balanced upon a pedestal of rock that jutted up from the sand. With a strength he did not possess while awake, Pánfilo inserted his mother between the boulder and the rock. When he had completed this sacred task, Pánfilo offered up a benediction: "Sleep, Mamá, sleep."

After a few moments of silence in honor of the dead, Pánfilo started his long trek back to the boat. The sun warmed his body and the gentle sand seeped through his toes with each step. But his serenity was dashed when the long-murdered Benedetti triplets captured him. They did cruel things to Pánfilo, things too ugly to describe. But he remained strong and cried for help but once.

Those Benedetti monsters! They are three evil bastards who deserved to be murdered! But even the atrocities they visited upon poor Pánfilo had to come to an end, more out of boredom than mercy. They released Pánfilo, bruised and bleeding, and told him to leave RIGHT THIS INSTANT or else they would begin again with their tortures. Pánfilo limped away as fast as his battered body would allow. But in his heart, he felt proud that he had laid his mother to rest.

Pánfilo made it to the boat, which seemed to be waiting for him like a loyal dog. He got in, sat down, and closed his eyes. Pánfilo could feel the boat move, sliding slowly across the vast lake in the direction from which he had come. He eventually felt a presence near the boat, floating out before him in the water. Pánfilo's eyes popped open and what he saw made him smile. A few yards from the boat's bow floated three figures amidst flotsam. Ah! There is justice! The three figures were none other than the Benedetti triplets, wrapped tightly in tarpaulins, surrounded by the malevolent debris of their short lives. The boat slid by the bodies and Pánfilo grinned in satisfaction.

In time, Pánfilo's boat reached the shore. His bruises and lacerations had miraculously healed, and he felt as fit as a young boy. He stepped out of the boat. The moment his left foot touched the sand, Pánfilo fell into darkness, fast and dizzying, deep, deep, deep into an abyss. And it is here that he saw his mother's face once more: elegant, loving, familiar. And Pánfilo smiled because he knew that she would be his mother forever.

Before Pánfilo hit bottom he awoke from his dream, a smile still upon his face. He sat up and looked around his small room. Pánfilo knew that he had shown the ultimate love for his mother, even though it was in a dream. He rubbed the sleep from his eyes and sat in silence. But then he realized that this would be his last dream. There would be no more. He knew this as well as he knew his own name. And with that, Pánfilo Velasco closed his eyes and wept.

Homecoming

Who had the toasted sesame seed bagel with butter?

He did, said Jacob pointing across the small table. I had the everything bagel with cream cheese.

The girl shifted her body and turned to Ramón, tossing her head back to get an unruly black curl off her forehead. It immediately fell back down. She wrinkled her nose in exasperation. She looked down at Ramón and froze. Her brown eyes widened, and then a broad smile took over her face revealing white teeth marred only by a silver bar running across them in parallel lines. Ramón returned the smile. Jacob sighed.

Thanks, Ida, said Ramón as he took the plate from the girl. It looks great.

She smiled. Sure.

Jacob cleared his throat but the girl kept staring at Ramón.

The other one is for me, Jacob finally said.

Ida blinked herself out of the trance and turned to Jacob. Sorry, she whispered as she handed Jacob his food.

No problem, said Jacob. It happens a lot.

Ramón let out a snicker. Ida blushed a deep red.

I'm sorry, she said trying to recover her composure. It's my first day back after summer vacation. It's odd seeing everyone again.

How's your dad? asked Ramón as he opened a napkin and put it on his lap.

Oh, smiled Ida, grateful for the small talk. Doing better. The doctor called it a minor heart attack and put Pop on a special diet. He has to exercise more, too. But he's a tough guy, right?

Right, said Ramón.

Ida stood in silence for a couple of seconds as if she were lost in thought. Jacob fidgeted with his plate but Ramón just sat smiling at the girl.

You look different, she finally said to Ramón.

In a bad way?

No, she said with another wave of red spreading over her face. Older, I guess.

Silence again. Ida remembered her job: Do you need anything else?

Actually, said Jacob. I could use some strawberry jam.

Ramón interrupted: No thanks. We're fine.

Ida nodded and went back behind the counter.

Jacob leaned closer to Ramón and whispered, If she only knew she was wasting her energies on you.

Ramón took a big bite out of his bagel. Mmmmm . . . was all he could get out as a response.

I mean, continued Jacob, how fair is that? I can't even get a date for Homecoming and Ida is giving you all her attention.

Ramón wiped his mouth. Jealous.

Yeah, and so?

Ramón took a gulp of his latte. Look, I can't help it that she finds me irresistible.

Yeah, said Jacob as he lifted the bagel to his mouth. But it's *every* hot girl we meet. Don't they have gaydar?

Maybe they do have gaydar and that's what turns them on.

Jacob looked over to Ida, who was helping a white-haired woman choose some bagels. She ignored Jacob's stare and glanced at Ramón, who offered her a big smile again.

Stop it, said Jacob. You're killing me.

Well, maybe if you acted queer you'd get more girls.

Jacob almost choked on his food. That's the stupidest thing you've said all week.

No, I mean it, said Ramón. Here, let me help.

Ramón reached over to Jacob's hand and patted it. Jacob almost jumped out of his seat and put his hands under the table. Ida's smile disappeared and she shook her head slowly. The white-haired woman pointed at the onion bagels and lifted two fingers.

Now you've ruined any chance I had with her, said Jacob.

You never had a chance with Ida, said Ramón. She's a sophomore.

It still isn't fair.

You know what's not fair?

Jacob didn't want to hear the lecture but he knew he had no choice.

What's not fair, said Ramón, is that you can't tell your parents that your best friend, the guy you've known since preschool, likes boys, not girls.

Jacob put up his left hand, palm toward Ramón. Do I have to hear this again?

And what's not fair is that every guy I think is hot turns out *not* to be gay, continued Ramón undeterred. And my parents don't want me to start dating yet because they're so afraid of HIV. Like I don't already know about safe sex. I mean Jesus Christ! It's goddamn 2004. We *all* know how to use condoms.

Okay, okay, said Jacob.

They act like every gay guy has AIDS.

At least your parents know who you are, said Jacob. My parents have no idea how I feel about anything. All they care about is that I get A's so that I can get into a great college. And whenever I get a little distracted, they ask me if I've forgotten to take my meds.

Ramón put the back of his hand on his forehead and looked up to the ceiling. Ay Dios mío, he said dramatically. Jacob's got big problems.

Jacob was on a roll: And I hate this fucking high school. It's so preppie and I can't stand wearing a shirt and tie every Friday for assembly. I feel like such an asshole.

Hey, cuties, may I sit? Is this seat taken?

Ramón and Jacob looked up simultaneously. Kayla stood above them, her hands clenched in little fists on her small hips.

Hey, said Jacob.

Hey, mi cielo, smiled Ramón.

May I sit? she asked again as she pulled out a chair. Or am I interrupting an intimate moment?

We're just having a lover's spat, said Ramón.

Stop it, fuck ass, said Jacob. Sit down, Kayla. Save me from this asshole.

Kayla plopped down with a little grunt. You want me here, boys. I've got some good gossip.

Oh? said Jacob as he took a bite of his bagel.

Come on, said Ramón. Spill the goods.

Kayla looked around to see if any of their friends were nearby. She saw Ida busy with the cash register and too far to hear. She patted her already perfect, short Afro and cleared her throat. She leaned over the table and whispered: Guess who's pregnant?

Jacob almost choked. What?

Ramón looked horrified. Someone we know?

Duh? said Kayla. Have any guesses?

Ramón and Jacob looked at each other. Neither answered.

Sonia.

No shit! said Ramón.

Jacob turned to Kayla and whispered: Are you sure?

I'm certain.

But it doesn't make sense.

What do you mean?

I mean, Jacob said, she's Catholic and all.

Kayla narrowed her eyes. That's one of the stupidest things you've ever said.

Calm down. You know what I mean.

Oh, said Kayla. So the Virgin Mary will keep all good Catholic girls from getting pregnant until they're safely married, right?

Jacob shook his head. You always take things the wrong way. Ramón, help me here.

Ramón shook his head and smiled.

Well, maybe you just say all the wrong things, Kayla said. Besides, I know more about why you had your bar mitzvah than you know about why I had my confirmation. You could try a little harder, you know.

Okay, what I meant was—

I know what you meant.

What I meant was Sonia always seemed to know how to take care of herself, said Jacob. I mean, she's a good student and she's really religious, too. So it doesn't make sense.

Sonia is really naive, said Kayla. That's how it could happen.

But are you certain?

Kayla let out a big breath. Totally certain. Alexi told me. And she's Sonia's best friend.

But what is she going to do?

Have you seen her at school this week?

Jacob thought for a moment. No, I don't think so.

Well, said Kayla, her parents already sent her down to Mexico to stay with cousins until the baby is born.

She's going to have the baby?

God! Kayla almost yelped. She's Catholic, remember?

But you said . . .

Okay, guys, said Ramón. Let's wait until we know more, right? Besides, we have something very important to deal with.

Fine, said Kayla. You're right. Alexi might be wrong.

So, what's more important? asked Jacob.

We need to plot, said Ramón.

Plot? asked Kayla.

Yes, Ramón said. None of us has a date for Homecoming, remember?

This is more important than Sonia? Jacob asked.

She's not pregnant, said Ramón. There is no fucking way she's pregnant.

I hope you're right, said Kayla.

But Homecoming is three weeks away, said Jacob. That's a lot of time.

Wrong, said Ramón. We have a lot of work to do. A *lot* of work.

Ramón reached for his backpack and pulled out a piece of paper and a black Sharpie. He slowly and neatly wrote each of their names in the left margin and drew three lines by each name.

What's that? Jacob asked.

Our future, said Ramón. Just waiting to be written.

You're writing my future? asked Jacob.

You'll thank me forever, said Ramón. I will be your hero.

Jacob rolled his eyes.

Oh ye of little faith, Ramón intoned.

Okay, sweetie, explain, said Kayla.

My pleasure, said Ramón.

Jacob said, Looks like a math problem.

Ramón took a drink from his latte and nodded. We need mathematical certainty.

For what? asked Jacob.

Homecoming dates, announced Ramón.

Ah! Kayla said.

Uh-oh, said Jacob.

Ramón stared at the paper for a moment and then wrote at the top in block letters: THE DATING GAME. He paused, thought for a moment, and then crossed out GAME and wrote in MATRIX.

Kayla's eyes widened. Okay, what do we do?

I don't know about this, Jacob said.

Calm down, said Ramón. Just hear me out.

Why?

Because if you don't have a date for Homecoming, not only will your freshman year be ruined, but you'll become a loser legend which will prevent you from ever getting a date your entire high school career.

Jacob shifted and coughed. Oh, he muttered. Why didn't you say so in the first place?

Sweetie, explain it please, begged Kayla.

Okay, here's how it works, said Ramón. On the left side are our names. To the right of each of our names we'll list at least three potential dates in order of preference, right?

Cool, smiled Kayla.

Jacob just stared at the paper.

You got a problem with it? asked Ramón.

Jacob took a drink and then slowly said: Any three names?

Yes, answered Ramón. I mean, within reason. You can't put Katie Holmes. Ain't gonna happen, you know.

I know, I know, Jacob said. But can I put a sophomore in my list?

Kayla grinned. Would that sophomore just happen to be working here?

Ramón turned serious. Kayla, that would be cruel. We have to be realistic.

Thanks for the vote of confidence, said Jacob.

Why can't he put Ida? said Kayla.

Not so loud, Jacob whispered. She'll hear you.

Kayla lowered her voice: Jake has every right to put Ida on his list. And I will do everything in my power to help him.

But there's another problem, said Ramón. Ida isn't Jewish and Jake's parents will not be happy.

It's a dance, not a fucking wedding, said Jacob. And let me deal with my parents, okay?

Clean up that mouth, said Kayla. Not the right way to woo someone like Ida, believe me.

Okay, fine, it's not a *darn* wedding. Better?

Perfect.

Ramón threw himself back in his chair and held up his hands in surrender. Fine. We'll put Ida down as your first choice.

And? prodded Kayla.

And I promise to do everything humanly possible a soccer hero can do to make certain she comes as your date to Homecoming. Happy?

As happy as a boy can be, said Jacob. But since when are you a soccer hero?

Ramón sighed. Okay, he said. I've put Ida down. Who's your second choice?

Tiffany, answered Jacob without hesitation. For some reason she hasn't been asked yet.

Ramón nodded his approval and wrote TIFFANY under IDA. He said: Definitely more in the realm of reality.

Stop it, Ramón, Kayla snapped.

Jacob stood up. I've got to use the bathroom.

You idiot, Kayla said. Why do you have to push him like that?

Ramón answered: He's used to it. That's how we relate.

But it's getting old, you know that? He's not exactly fitting in at high school and you're just reminding him of that.

Ramón sighed as he threw the marker on the table. It clacked on the wood and then bounced to the floor. I'm an idiot.

Yep.

So how do I de-idiot myself?

Kayla reached down and snatched up the marker. Just encourage him a little, okay?

Okay.

He's coming back. Try. Please.

Jacob sat down slowly. I guess you're right, Ramón.

What do you mean?

Ida is out of my league.

Kayla nudged Ramón.

No, she's not, he said to Jacob. Actually, I think she's a distinct possibility.

Stop shitting me, said Jacob in a flat voice.

No, I mean it. In fact, I've thought of a third name for you.

Jacob sat up. Really?

Yep.

Kayla eyed Ramón suspiciously. Who is it?

Amanda, Ramón announced clearly proud of himself.

Amanda? Jacob said in wonder. She doesn't have a date yet?

Everyone's too afraid to ask her, answered Ramón. And she's Jewish.

Put her down now, said Jacob. That's a great list.

Kayla nodded, impressed.

Now we turn to la chica más bonita, cooed Ramón. What stud goes first by your name?

Just then, Ida walked up to them. What're you guys working on? she asked, trying to decipher the diagram.

Ramón snatched up the paper and held it to his chest. Top secret, Ida. For our eyes only.

Oh, she said. Didn't mean to intrude.

But, said Ramón, we were just talking about Homecoming.

Jacob tried to signal to Ramón with rapidly blinking eyes to stop this line of conversation, but to no avail.

We're going to triple date, continued Ramón. Rent a limo, go as a group. Do you have plans?

No, I don't have a date yet.

Well, said Ramón, it just so happens that Jake here has been so busy with honors biology and English that he hasn't had a chance to ask anyone yet. And he would be flattered if you came with him.

Ida looked between Jacob and then Ramón and then back to Jacob. Finally, she said: It'll be a triple date?

Yep, smiled Ramón. Six friends, one limo, a fantastic night of dancing. Ramón kicked Jacob's foot.

Yes, said Jacob. I'd be honored. With that, he stood.

Ida thought for a moment. She turned to Kayla: So you're going, too? Wouldn't miss it.

After another moment, Ida said, Yes, I'd love to go.

Jacob almost jumped out of his shoes. Cool! he said. We'll talk more about the logistics and all.

Ida nodded. Yeah. I have to get back to the counter, she said as she walked away.

Jacob sat slowly. He couldn't believe what just happened.

Ramón gloated. Kayla patted him on the back.

One down, said Ramón as he put the piece of paper back on the table, and two to go.

Ramón took in the cool evening air as he walked slowly down the street. He liked this time, when he could be alone. He allowed the sounds of the neighborhood to wash over him hoping they would make his thoughts smooth, easy, orderly. A terrier's high-pitched barking through the large bay window at Mr. Komen's house. About a dozen cawing crows circling, plotting their next move. Children laughing, shouting as they ran home for dinner. Leaves rustling in the autumn wind sounding like crisp, new crinoline. This was Ramón's time, after a tough soccer practice and a hot shower, his muscles aching while feeling strong. But tonight these sounds didn't seem to help make sense of his thoughts. He tried to take them one at a time, but they came at him like annoying flies, without order, relentless.

There was the subject of Sonia. Ramón hoped that Alexi was wrong. But if she was pregnant, how must she feel, shuttled off to Mexico to have her baby. The last time he saw Sonia was at Sunday Mass in early August before school started. She looked fine, even happy. Ramón remembered what she wore: a yellow-and-blue cotton summer dress, cinched tight at the waist with a white belt. She looked beautiful. But she must have known by then, right? If she was pregnant, there was no way Sonia could have gone to Mass that day, taken Holy Communion, and not known that she was going to be a mother early the next year. But her waist was so tiny. Wouldn't she have been showing by then? Maybe Sonia had to go to Mexico because of a family emergency. But Alexi was never wrong. She always had the facts. Ramón shook his head and tried not to think about it. He needed to think of something else.

Homecoming. Jacob had the date of his dreams even though Ida probably was more excited about being in the same limo with Ramón than being Jacob's date. But the DATING MATRIX didn't fill out very well for Kayla. Of course, she put Ramón's name down as a safe choice, and he put Kayla's down as well. After all, they'd attended so many dances together that those who didn't suspect that Ramón was gay thought they were a couple. He remembered all the times they went together: Jacob's bar mitzvah, Ramón's cousin's quinceañera, the graduation party. They never failed to have lots of fun. Ramón and Kayla were always the best dancers on the floor, and he made certain she felt special. Sometimes he wished he were straight or even bi. Life would be simpler that way. Once after a slow dance, she kissed him on the lips. And Ramón kissed back. But no tongues. Just a soft, sweet kiss. But then he whispered to Kayla: You're my best friend. Friend. That's it. Nothing more.

But they knew this couldn't go on forever. Kayla had decided to add another name to the DATING MATRIX: Hunter. She and Ramón had known Hunter Caine all through elementary school, and now they had almost every class together. He was not as tall as Ramón, but Hunter had those sparkling green eyes and thick, light brown curls. Hunter wasn't known to date a lot but everyone knew he was kind of shy. Why not put him down? So Kayla did. Jacob thought he was a good choice. But Ramón had said: Hunter? He's so, what's the word? Boring. What could be worse than boring? Ramón's verdict came out like a challenge. So Kayla had said: Yes, Hunter. He's cute and smart. I want to put him as my first choice, before you, in fact. This last decision had startled Ramón. But he smiled and complied by making a red arrow on the DATING MATRIX that showed Hunter should be before him on the grid.

The odd thing was Ramón didn't put down another choice for himself. Only Kayla's name sat across from his. What if Hunter and I go together? Kayla had asked. For once Ramón didn't have a snappy answer. He'd merely shrugged his shoulders and said: Time for dinner. My parents are probably waiting for me.

After dinner and homework, Ramón surfed the web. He really wanted to call Kayla just to hear her voice and apologize. He looked at the news headlines which just made him more depressed: a huge earthquake on the other side of the world, the never-ending war, President Bush wearing a goofy grin and predicting his reelection. Ramón looked for some new songs and videos. But this was wrong. He should IM Kayla.

> BUSYBOY: whattup?
> KAYLA3: nm. u?
> BUSYBOY: same.
> KAYLA3: bored?
> BUSYBOY: what else?
> KAYLA3: question . . .
> BUSYBOY: out with it, mi cielo.
> KAYLA3: hunter.
> BUSYBOY: yes . . .
> KAYLA3: boring?
> BUSYBOY: nah. not really.
> KAYLA3: sure?
> BUSYBOY: totally.
> KAYLA3: why you say so then?

Ramón paused for several moments. He envisioned Kayla at her laptop, lounging on her bed, waiting for a response. Then he answered.

BUSYBOY: cuz i'm stupid.
KAYLA3: LOL!
BUSYBOY: i can always make you laugh.
KAYLA3: yep, sweetie.
BUSYBOY: i'm da best.
KAYLA3: 2 much for me.
BUSYBOY: como no.
KAYLA: yawn!
BUSYBOY: time for sleep.
KAYLA3: yes.
BUSYBOY: g2g.:-6
KAYLA3: me 2.
BUSYBOY: sleep tight, mi cielo.
KAYLA3: night night.:-*
BUSYBOY::**:

On Monday morning, Ramón fiddled with his combination lock as he tried to remember the order of his morning classes. Middle school had been so easy. Now everything was so much more complicated. A rotating schedule, six different teachers, way more books, too much distance between classrooms. He had promised himself that he'd memorize his classes before the semester even started, but here it was the third week of high school and he completely blanked on what he had this morning. Ramón prayed that he had an extra schedule lying at the bottom of his locker. Finally, the lock clicked and the locker opened with a *creak*. But what met Ramón was a horrible smell.

Damn, boy, what died in there?

Ramón turned to his left and saw Hunter Caine two lockers away. Ramón reached into his locker and pulled out a soggy paper bag.

Crap! said Hunter as he held his nose. Smells like rancid tuna!

Two girls walked by and simultaneously let out a *Gross!* as they scurried away from the stench. Ramón held the bag with two fingers far from his body.

Actually, it's worse, said Ramón while trying to breathe through his mouth. Cheese and bean burrito.

Shit, man!

Ramón searched left and right and finally spied a trashcan about three yards away. He took aim and then successfully flung the bag into the trash. It made a sick, mushy thump when it landed.

Two points! cheered Hunter. You could trade in your soccer cleats for a basketball uniform.

Sorry about that, said Ramón as he rifled through his locker for a schedule. Bingo! he exclaimed when he found it.

We've got English first period today, Hunter said as he gathered up several books. And then biology, ceramics, and then, thank God, lunch.

Hunter perused the inside of his locker one more time before slamming it closed. Ramón pulled out his books but didn't close his.

I wish I could air this thing out, said Ramón as he sniffed the air in disgust.

Gotta close that baby up, said Hunter as he walked toward Ramón. No option.

Ramón sighed. Slowly he closed his locker until it clicked.

We're going to be late for English, Hunter said. Let's walk.

Ramón nodded and they started off across the yard.

I didn't know we had so many classes together, said Ramón.

Yep.

Ramón realized that this was his chance to help Kayla. But how could he broach the subject so it didn't seem obvious? Maybe the best strategy was just to jump in with both feet and forget about the consequences.

Going to Homecoming? asked Ramón without looking at Hunter.

Well, mused Hunter, that's kind of complicated.

How so?

Hunter coughed. I don't know.

Ramón saw an opening.

You know Kayla? he asked.

Hunter thought for a moment. Yeah, she's your friend. Real pretty.

Yeah, smiled Ramón finally turning toward Hunter. Hunter was already staring right at Ramón.

Aren't you taking her? asked Hunter. I mean, you guys seem so close. All through middle school you guys always went to the dances together.

Kayla and I are real good friends, but she kind of wants to go to Homecoming with someone else. I mean, it's like, she wants it to be special.

Hunter laughed. Hey, you're special.

Ramón ignored the comment and pushed on with his strategy.

Kayla is so cute and she's smart, too, Ramón argued. I think any guy would be lucky to go with her to Homecoming.

True, said Hunter.

I suspect she wouldn't mind if you asked her, Ramón ventured.

Hunter scratched his nose and remained quiet for a moment. The bell rang just as they got to the classroom. Mr. Nguyen already stood at the blackboard writing the theme for today's class: *The Metaphor*. Hunter walked to the back of the class and found his desk. Ramón automatically followed him.

Let's talk later, said Hunter as he sat down. Cool?

Cool.

Ramón turned and walked to his assigned desk at the front of the class. He felt a little stupid not realizing that Hunter was in three of his classes. But it didn't matter. More important, did Ramón successfully plant a seed in Hunter's brain that would eventually lead to him asking Kayla to Homecoming?

———————————

Hunter and Ramón strode across the yard toward their next class. Hunter jumped right back into the conversation. He no longer seemed shy.

Look, I think Kayla is a great girl, he said.

Ramón nodded in agreement. So?

Well, she's not exactly my type.

Ramón stopped walking. What?

Hunter turned to face Ramón. It's not a big deal or anything.

What do you mean by type?

Hey, said Hunter pulling back a step. I didn't mean anything by it.

Wrong color maybe?

No! Hunter almost yelled. I'm not like that! That's not what I meant!

What else could you have meant?

Look, said Hunter in a more controlled voice. It's all so complicated.

What's complicated about a great-looking girl with brains who wants a date for Homecoming?

It's like this, began Hunter. I've never really had a girlfriend before.

Sorry I jumped all over you, said Ramón. It just seemed like you were saying something else.

I know, laughed Hunter. I said it kind of stupidly. If I were you, I'd have gotten mad, too.

They started walking again toward class. Ramón searched his mind for something to say to salvage the conversation.

Well, if Kayla isn't your type, who is? he finally asked.

My type? asked Hunter softly.

Yeah.

There was a long silence filled only by the other students' shouts and laughs.

You, Hunter said. *You.*

Ramón almost tripped. The bell rang.

We're going to be late, said Hunter. Let's hurry.

Hunter broke into a trot. Ramón couldn't move his legs. Fuck, he thought. Fuck.

———————————

Ramón felt as though he had betrayed Kayla when he agreed to meet Hunter after soccer practice. Behind the science bungalows near the high chain-link fence, Hunter's note had said, a note he had slipped onto Ramón's desk at end of their last class. But why feel guilty? Ramón hadn't done anything. In fact, he was trying to help Kayla. Besides, there were plenty of straight guys who would die to go out with her. How many gay guys—guys who were out, guys who were cute and smart—were there for Ramón to choose from? No. No need for guilt.

Ramón swung his gym bag back and forth as he slowly walked toward the bungalows. His hair was still wet from the shower, and he shivered a bit as a slight breeze blew across the yard. Most of the students had left campus; the bungalows always emptied out first because they sat far from the school's parking lot and main office. As Ramón approached, he squinted into the sun. Where was Hunter? Ah! There, by the fence, leaning against the ancient eucalyptus tree. Hunter. He *was* pretty cute.

Hey, said Hunter when Ramón came within six feet of him.

Ramón stopped. Something wasn't right. He heard the crackle of dried leaves behind him. He turned and there stood another boy, someone he didn't recognize, bigger and older than both Hunter and Ramón. The boy snickered. He held a two-foot-long metal bar in his right hand, hanging loosely by his side. Ramón turned to Hunter.

Hey, faggot, whispered Hunter. Need a date for Homecoming?

Ramón heard the boy behind him take a step, a slow, deliberate crunch.

Ramón swung his gym bag around. The boy jumped back and dropped the metal bar with a loud *Oh, shit!* Ramón let the bag circle above his head and then let it fly high toward the fence. Hunter and the boy watched, confused, as the projectile arced perfectly, beautifully, over the top. And that's when Ramón made his move. He broke into a sprint toward the fence, keeping his eyes at its highest point, nine feet from the ground. He heard cussing, first Hunter, then the boy. But he kept focused, his legs and arms pumping, hands in tight fists. He jumped, right toe taking hold into the chain link, arms up, fingers linking into the crosshatched metal.

And then he felt two hands grab his dangling left foot. Ramón didn't need to think what to do. He kicked, heel out, hard, with his strong, soccer-trained muscles almost acting on their own. Once, twice, and then a third kick connected with something hard, a cracking sound, a muffled scream, his foot now free. Ramón clung tightly to the fence, turned in time to watch Hunter fall onto his back, his eyes bulging, mouth working, jaw crooked, face unnatural. The older boy yelled *Shit!* and turned to run. When the boy was a safe distance away, Ramón jumped from his perch, feet landing near Hunter's shaking body. And then Ramón saw it: a shard of white jaw bone jutting from Hunter's skin, remarkably little blood coming from the wound. Hunter continued to make a sickening, muffled sound, part moan, part scream.

Ramón pulled his cell phone from his shirt pocket, flipped it open, but then froze. Hunter's eyes pleaded: *Call for help!* Ramón closed his own eyes, his breathing heavy. That sound, that sound . . . he wished Hunter would stop making that sound. After a few moments he opened his eyes and punched in 9-1-1. And as he spoke with the dispatcher, Ramón turned from Hunter and looked toward the fence. The sun was setting just beyond the tall trees across the street. The tinny dispatcher's voice told him what to do until the ambulance came. And at that moment a soft breeze blew through the yard. Ramón thought that he'd never seen a sunset more beautiful.

Meeting with My Editor

I am meeting with my editor, right now, as you read this story, a meeting *about* this story that I first submitted to her rather prestigious literary journal, a literary journal that will remain nameless, but one that has published three of my stories, two of which won Pushcarts. So she feels like she has dibs on me and my little successes. We're discussing a story that she asked for but now is questioning whether it's exactly what she had in mind.

She says: This isn't exactly what I had in mind.

What did you have in mind? I ask before taking a sip of iced tea. I like this restaurant, Pete's Café, on Main Street in the Old Bank District. This part of downtown L.A. is really bustling now that these wonderful early-1900s office and bank buildings have been converted to mixed-use lofts. New eateries, little markets, bars, hair salons. Pete's Café was one of the first to open, about ten years ago, but it's owned by one of the bigger loft developers so he (the developer, not Pete since there's no Pete as far as I know) has skin in the game, as they say.

She picks at her tuna niçoise salad while keeping her eyes on mine. I couldn't do that. I need to look at my food when I pick at it. She sighs.

Something with more, I don't know, more, you know, ethnicity.

Excuse me?

She leans closer to me, lowers her voice because now she sees that I'm annoyed.

Your stories usually focus on Chicano characters, you know, dealing with, uh, you know . . .

Chicano things?

Yes! she chirps. I wanted more culture in the story, and maybe a bit more plot, she adds.

I look down at my Thai turkey burger. It's goddamn good, smothered in peanut sauce and some apricot-pineapple chutney, a side of sweet potato fries. But this editor is ruining it.

Okay, I say, reaching over and snatching my story from her side of the table. I grab a Sharpie from my shirt pocket, open it, and say with a flourish: How about if I cut out the first paragraph for starters, like this:

> ~~I am meeting with my editor, right now, as you read this story, a meeting about this story that I submitted to her rather prestigious literary journal, a literary journal that will remain unnamed, but one that has published three of my stories, two of which won Pushcarts. So she feels like she has dibs on me and my little successes. We're discussing a story that she asked for but now is questioning whether it's exactly what she had in mind.~~

She blinks slowly, then narrows her eyes.

And then I say, how about I begin with this, and she watches as I quickly write this in the white space above the paragraph I just struck:

> *"¡Chingada!" Ernesto yelled as his thin body fell down hard on the blacktop after missing the layup. His white skin almost glowed in the harsh afternoon sunlight and his light brown hair glistened like a halo. Ernesto's face was almost pretty except for the numerous deep scars on his right cheek and near his chin.*

I hand it to her and she reads to herself. She smiles when done. I like that! she says.

Can't have it, I say and snatch it back again. The waiter comes by and refills my glass. He reminds me of Peter O'Toole, who just died the other day. He was born the same year my parents were: 1932. But my parents are still ticking, knock on wood. We wait until he leaves before we start up again.

Why not? she asks. It's exactly what I want.

Because I wrote it years ago and it's in my first short-story collection.

She drops her fork into her salad, reaches for her purse, and throws some money on the table before standing and whispering: You're an asshole, you know? Before I can answer, she turns and leaves Pete's.

I look down at the bills and notice that she hasn't left enough to cover her share of the tab. Whatever. So I pull up the story on my Android and submit it to this literary journal, the one you now hold. I think it'd be a good fit. And, to be honest, this journal is more prestigious than *her* journal. I lift my burger and take a big bite. It's a bit cold, but it still tastes fucking good. I like Pete's. I say out loud: Long live Pete's!

Gig Economy

The young lawyer stands on the sidewalk outside the Ronald Reagan State Building on Spring Street. He hums, swings his briefcase from side to side, pleased with himself, waiting for his Uber to arrive and whisk him off to the Burbank Airport. The Los Angeles afternoon sun makes his already damp dress shirt adhere to the soft contours of his torso. He's gained another ten pounds in the last two months, the late nights at the large San Francisco firm combined with takeout Chinese, Thai, and Mexican food all taking a toll on his once lean body. But he is successful, getting top performance reviews from the partners, veiled promises of great things to come in his career. Few young associates would get the opportunity to argue an appellate case as he just did, on an important contract dispute that could make great authority if the court sides with him and issues a favorable published opinion, creating *stare decisis*—a decision that will be cited by the legal treatises, taught in law schools, relied upon by other attorneys in their briefs.

The Uber arrives and the young lawyer hops into the backseat of the odd-looking car. Not a wreck, merely a dark green, boxy, generic vehicle without a hint of personality. The driver turns to him—a woman old enough to be his grandmother—smiles, and winks. The gig economy has opened up opportunities for everyone, he thinks, even for older folks on fixed incomes. He smiles back and fastens his seatbelt in time for the woman to screech away from the government building.

The young lawyer snaps open his briefcase—a graduation gift from his father, a man who never finished high school but who worked several jobs to make certain his only child could go to college and then law school, something the man and his late wife never could have imagined when they surreptitiously crossed the border into the United States twenty-eight years ago, a young, brave couple who wanted to make a better life for themselves and their soon-to-be-born child in this land of opportunity.

Such a shame the man's wife would not survive a brazen, selfish cancer that took her away before their son graduated from law school three years ago.

As the young lawyer rifles through his briefcase, he notices the car has stopped. He looks up and sees brick walls on either side of him. An alley. The woman turns to him, winks, and holds up a finger as if to say: One moment, please. She pops the trunk, hops out, and scurries to the back of the car. The young lawyer shrugs—he has plenty of time before his flight—and resumes his rifling.

After a few minutes the young lawyer starts to perspire. The woman probably did not leave the air conditioning on as she searched for God-knows-what in her trunk. But wait: the young lawyer can hear the car's vents going full blast, but it's hot air, not cold, pouring out. He sighs, snaps shut his brief case, and reaches for the door handle. He pulls, but nothing happens. He tries again. And again nothing. He scooches over the unusually hard plastic seat to the other door and tries that one, but no success. The young lawyer looks for the door lock but sees smooth plastic where a latch should be. It is getting unbearably hot. He loosens his tie just as the woman slams shut the trunk.

The young lawyer's breathing becomes labored. He turns to search for the woman. She is behind the car, looking at the young lawyer, sharpening a glistening carving knife on a black, rectangular stone. She licks her lips, smiles, winks.

Just as the young lawyer begins to lose consciousness, his mind drifts back to his first day of kindergarten. His beautiful mother walks him up to the school's gate, his sweaty little hand in hers. She squats, her perfume fills the air with love, and touches her anxious son's cheek. Mi cielo, she coos, I love you. Do well and be good. Make us proud.

The Three Mornings of
José Antonio Rincón

It is true that if pressed, José Antonio Rincón would have denied enjoying the experience because, regardless of the changes he endured during those three days last April, his basic nature remained the same. That is to say, José Antonio was, is, and will always be a contrarian. During his almost six decades of life on this earth his contrarian nature only grew stronger each year, with roots as reliable and resilient as those of a northern red oak. So if you asked him, did you like it, José Antonio? Was it pleasant? He no doubt would frown, purse his lips, and shout, "No, it was hellish!" However, if you said: Oh, what horrors! How did you survive it all? He very likely would smile and say it was all quite delightful, and he would sincerely express his hope that it should happen again and again and again.

And so it was one Monday morning—on April 8 of last year to be exact—that José Antonio woke to his radio alarm with *Morning Edition*'s Steve Inskeep and Renée Montagne informing him of the day's headlines. But he did not quite feel himself.

No, wait, this is not what you think. I am not telling you a fairy tale of metamorphoses similar to that other writer's famous story. No, not at all. I do not steal, not even when it would be undemanding. That other narrative involved one poor man's transformation into vermin. My story does not. ¡Ay Dios mio! I cannot stand small, crawling insects. Ni modo. My account is not woven from imagination; it actually occurred. José Antonio Rincón is a dear friend of mine, a man I've known for almost fifteen years, a personage I've observed year in and year out as he worked in the cubicle across from mine at the government agency that shall remain nameless because I am not a brave man and I do not want to ruin steady employment and a solid pension. In sum, what I am saying to you is this:

My story is based in fact, not fancy, and I do not steal stories from others, especially not from dead foreigners with big ears.

As I was saying, while José Antonio lay on his back that Monday morning last year, stirring to the sounds of his radio alarm tuned to his favorite public radio station—the one he fails to support with donations during the fund drives that he particularly enjoys listening to because he enjoys getting things for free—his stomach rumbled louder than usual, which prompted him to spread his palms on what normally would have been a respectable paunch earned through years of steady employment and hearty lunches eaten during the work week with yours truly. Instead, José Antonio's splayed fingers felt the contours of well-defined abdominal muscles, those of a young man who went to the gym more times per week than José Antonio went in his lifetime . . . think Brad Pitt or Benjamin Bratt. He jumped out of bed—just as Renée Montagne explained how the Mexican government had agreed to release additional water into the Rio Grande from its tributaries outside of a seventy-nine-year-old water rights treaty in response to a devastating drought—and ran to the full-length mirror in the corner of his rather capacious bedroom. José Antonio lifted his pajama top and gazed upon perfectly cut abs, those of a young male model. How could it be?

But then he noticed it . . . well, not it—a person is not an "it"—but the rest of himself. Where a paunchy, middle-aged, though pleasant-looking man should have been staring back from the mirror's surface, José Antonio focused his eyes on what could only be described as a Chicano Adonis! Better than Pitt or Bratt—if you can imagine such a thing!—he had transformed into another being.

Now, many questions are likely running through your mind, as they did mine when José Antonio told me this. Rather than spend time answering them, I would prefer to describe what he did next because, as you well know when it comes to storytelling, it is better to show rather than tell. But I do want to be sensitive to your needs . . . I know that you are short on time, a busy person you are, of course, with many places to visit, various people to see. Let me use simple bullet points as I delineate what my dear friend José Antonio Rincón did next:

- José Antonio called his supervisor and, in the best sick-sounding croak he could muster, told her that he had caught that flu that was going around the office. She wished him well and recommended that he take the rest of the week off, particularly since he had accrued much too much annual leave credits which needed to be used before he hit the maximum of 640 hours and then—well, there would be hell to pay.

- José Antonio showered (allowing his hands to linger on his wonderful new body) and then shaved his dazzling face.

- José Antonio examined his closet wondering if anything would fit. Miraculously, when he donned his best wool slacks and a crisp cotton shirt, they slid onto his limbs as if they had been tailored for his new taller, trimmer body.

- José Antonio cooked a delicious breakfast of chorizo and scrambled eggs just as his late wife, Aimee, had done for him each morning for the short ten years they had together.

- José Antonio then drove to the Westfield Topanga Mall in the west San Fernando Valley so as to stay as far as possible from his downtown office; he walked about the mall for several hours allowing many women and a few men to admire his newfound beauty.

- Once exhausted with "strutting his stuff"—as we used to say—José Antonio drove home and ate a simple lunch of wheat bread, sliced turkey, lettuce, and mayonnaise. He stripped down to his boxers and got into bed for a short nap.

Unfortunately for my friend, fatigue overtook his new body in such a manner that his nap was not short. Rather, José Antonio slumbered for fifteen hours! Perhaps his new physical manifestation was extremely taxing on his system. Ah, who knows. But what did happen next only made his life much stranger.

For you see, my friends, José Antonio Rincón woke the next morning in yet another body! Oh, as he told me this part of the story, I blinked and coughed and wiped my brow with a handkerchief (something most men no longer carry but which I believe is a sign of true elegance, not to mention the height of function). Yes, I was speechless but he immediately sensed what I wanted to ask and offered this answer: "I was no longer the Adonis but, rather, I had transformed into a somewhat handsome older woman, perhaps sixty years of age, short but solidly built, not corpulent, but muscular, like a woman who had been an athlete in youth and still maintained healthful activities."

So, sitting in his boxers, José Antonio had a simple breakfast of oatmeal and black coffee (looking down at his new breasts and thinking them quite nice), showered (again allowing his hands to linger, this time in places he had not felt since Aimee had passed away), and searched his closet. This time he slipped into lightweight khaki trousers and a green Polo shirt that perfectly fit his shorter, broad-hipped new body.

Where did he go this time? Well, José Antonio thought about it for approximately twenty minutes, attempting to listen to his new body—if that is even possible—and then it came to him: A pleasant hike on the trails of Griffith Park, nothing too difficult, just enough to enjoy the great beauty of the area while getting a bit of exercise. I love that area, which has been compared to New York's Central Park, though Griffith Park is much larger and certainly more untamed and rugged. In any event, José Antonio found a pair of tattered tennis shoes in the back of the closet (again, they fit perfectly despite his smaller feet) and packed a small bag with bottled water and several granola bars.

Oh, what an enchanting time he had! José Antonio drove up to the Griffith Observatory—which, as you know, sits atop the southern slope of Mount Hollywood—and walked the trails that undulate like a dusty snake around that great astronomical structure that was featured prominently in the 1955 classic, *Rebel Without a Cause*. Indeed, José Antonio spent a few moments contemplating the bronze bust of the film's star, the late, great James Dean, before beginning his trek. Other than a few nods to other hikers, José Antonio said barely a word the entire day he was at the park. And again, when he got home hours later, he needed a nap and fell onto his bed without even removing his clothes.

José Antonio woke that third morning—not even needing *Morning Edition*—sprang out of bed, and scrambled to the mirror. But this time, as he looked at his reflection he saw his old self. Well, not exactly. Yes, his face and body looked as they had Sunday night, but there was something different around the eyes . . . a clarity, an added intelligence. This is not to say that José Antonio is an obtuse man. No, not all. In fact, I must say that I consider him my intellectual superior. He can as easily offer casual discourse on hermeneutics and Hempel's paradox as I can on jazz music and which wine to serve with zucchini linguine in a light herb sauce (an Austrian Grüner Veltliner, if you must know). What did he do? Well, José

Antonio dispensed with his usual shower. Rather, he stripped off his dusty clothes, put on a robe, prepared a large pot of coffee, and sat down to write three letters.

Letters? Oh, what a puzzlement! But as he explained further, I soon understood. Again, let me show, not tell:

The first letter he addressed to President Obama. In it, he explained in exquisite and quite logical detail how to achieve peace in the Middle East.

Next, he wrote to Dr. Tom Frieden, the director of the Centers for Disease Control and Prevention, offering nothing less than the chemical blueprint for the cure of most cancers.

Finally, José Antonio wrote a letter to me, his best friend. In it—well, I would rather not share its contents. Suffice it to say it made tears come to my eyes. I have never read a more beautiful declaration of friendship.

Once done—a good two hours and one whole pot of coffee later—José Antonio showered, shaved, and dressed so that he could make a quick trip to the post office. Once he had mailed the letters he came home and reread his three favorite books (in an astounding five hours' time):

> Tomás Rivera: The Complete Works
> Modern Latin America (the fifth edition, of course)
> Dictionary of Theories

Once he closed the cover on the third book, José Antonio yawned, leaned back in his large stuffed chair, and fell into a deep sleep.

The next morning he woke to find that he was himself again.

Is that the end of my tale? Well, not quite. After coming back to work the next week and telling me of his experiences, José Antonio decided to take early retirement, sell his home, and move to a little town in Mexico called Dos Cuentos. Perhaps you have heard of it. In any event, that was almost three months ago. I receive e-mails from him almost every day. He is quite content writing a book based on his experiences of those three days in April. The title of his tome? What else could it be? He calls it, *The Three Mornings of José Antonio Rincón*, and he has maybe another fifty more pages left to write. I have little doubt that it will be published—he has shared several chapters with me, and I must say, my friend has quite a charming writing style—though José Antonio admits that he will have to call it "fiction" otherwise he will be rejected by the publishing industry as a lunatic.

So, when his lovely novel does come out, please look for it in bookstores and remember that it is based on truth. And if you do not believe it, no matter. A story is a story. Nothing more, nothing less.

The Great Wall

Rogelio stood in the long line that snaked from the detention center's barracks to the lookout point at the other end of the compound. He shifted from foot to foot, the heat making him perspire and feel lightheaded. He was a smart boy—one of the best students in Ms. Becerra's fifth grade class—so he figured that even though the cool winter weather still made San Diego's evenings chilly enough to need a sweater, the lack of circulation combined with the body heat of thousands of children conspired to make the detention center's air heavy and almost suffocating.

The guards strolled slowly up and down the lines in an attempt to keep some order. But the children had become so numb to seeing the green-clad, rifle-bearing men and women that the best the guards could hope for was an organized chaos as the two lines—one for boys, the other girls—inched forward to the dual lookout points. Rogelio could see his older sister, Marisol, directly to his right in the girls' line. She comforted a younger girl who wept silently into Marisol's shoulder. Rogelio didn't like crying in front of his sister, but right then he wished Marisol had an arm around him whispering, "Don't worry. It'll be okay. We'll see mamá and papá soon."

Above the din of the other children, Rogelio could make out the recurring audio loop of the President's voice blaring over the intercoms that dotted the ceiling like so many menacing dark stars. He could almost recite those words from memory: "I will build a great wall—and nobody builds walls better than me, believe me—and I'll build them very inexpensively. I will build a great, great wall on our southern border, and I will make Mexico pay for that wall. Mark my words."

Rogelio had never seen the wall except online and on TV. He thought it was ugly even though the President had it decorated with an ornate, gold paint that swirled in strange designs along the wall's top and bottom edges. Between the borders of gold paint were bas-relief scenes from the

President's life beginning from his childhood, through school, beginning careers in business and television, running for president, the swearing in, and the President signing executive orders.

The children who had already visited the lookout points—which were simply large rooms with the far wall made of bulletproof Plexiglas—said that it would have been easier to set up computer screens to say goodbye to their parents. But, instead, the President's executive order explicitly prohibited the expenditure of funds for such "niceties" and, instead, ordered that the families' farewell would be soundless, without the aid of microphones, with children on one side of the Plexiglas, the parents on the other.

Once in the lookout points—one for boys, the other for girls, as decreed by the President—the children would wave to their parents who would be allowed to wave back. After a "humane" period of thirty seconds, the children would be directed out of the lookout point and back to their barracks to pack up their meager belongings for a new life with a relative or adopted family. Since these children had been born in the country, they were citizens. But their parents had entered the United States without documents, most with the assistance of well-paid coyotes. So, after the silent goodbyes, the parents would be ushered into a large, black bus that would whisk them off to one of the reinforced gates in the great wall and back to Mexico, even if they had come from a different Latin-American country. Neat, clean, fast, and beautiful.

As Rogelio inched closer to the boys' lookout point, his heart began to beat hard in his small chest. He willed himself not to cry, to be strong, to show his parents that he and his sister would be okay living with this aunt in Los Angeles who had become a United States citizen under President Reagan's 1986 Immigration Reform and Control Act.

The guard's loud "Next!" broke Rogelio's reverie. He walked into the lookout point and stepped up to the thick, cloudy Plexiglas. Rogelio squinted. About thirty yards of open terrain separated the two detention centers and their respective lookout points. Where were his parents? Oh, there! He could discern his father, who was a hearty, large man, but who now looked so small. His father wiped his eyes with a crumpled, white handkerchief, and embraced Rogelio's mother with his right arm. Rogelio's sister must have already seen their parents since she had been just a bit farther ahead in the girls' line. He wondered if Marisol had cried. But Rogelio promised himself that he would not. He waved to his parents as he forced a smile that looked more like a pained grimace. His parents waved back, also forcing smiles, but Rogelio could see that their faces were shiny with tears.

Before a guard directed his parents toward the exit, Rogelio let out a sob, his chest shaking without control. He told himself: *Don't cry, don't cry.* But now Rogelio's tears fell freely from his eyes as a guard put a hand on the boy's shoulder and gently guided him away.

Acknowledgments

Though I will never possess suitable eloquence or sufficient time to thank all who have helped make my latest book a reality, I will attempt to do so:

I am grateful to the wonderful and dedicated people at the University of Arizona Press who gave my manuscript this opportunity to come to life. Your dedication to Latino/a and Chicano/a literature is cherished by writers and readers alike.

Many thanks to those lovely editors of the literary journals and anthologies that first published many of these stories. I specifically and proudly acknowledge your publications, by name, at the end of this book.

A big Chicano abrazo to the many talented and dedicated authors who have encouraged and inspired my literary life. And as I have done before, I offer additional thanks to my fellow blogueros y blogueras of *La Bloga* who never fail to offer communal support for our strange vocation.

As for my day job, I thank my friends at the California Department of Justice who have read my books and attended my various book readings. You continue to help me integrate my life as a lawyer with that of an author. You have also inspired some of the fiction in this collection, especially "Good Things Happen at Tina's Café."

I thank my parents, who always made certain that we were a family of books and that we liberally used our library cards. You taught your children that there is joy in creating art, delight in reading, and magic in the written word.

Finally, I thank my wife, Susan Formaker, and our son, Benjamin Formaker-Olivas. I am nothing without you. I hope that you enjoy my new book, which I dedicate to you.

Credits

The following stories appeared previously, sometimes in slightly different form, in the following publications:

"Silver Case" (*Vestal Review*, 2000)
"Imprints" (*Southern Cross Review*, 2002)
"La Diabla at the Farm" (*LatinoLA*, 2004)
"Fat Man" (under the title "You were once a fat man . . .") (*Pindeldyboz*, 2005)
"Juana" (*PALABRA*, 2007)
"Kind of Blue" (*Antique Children*, 2009)
"Orange Line" (*The Coachella Review*, 2009)
"Better Than Divorce" (*Hint Fiction: An Anthology of Stories in 25 Words or Fewer*, W. W. Norton, 2010)
"Things We Do Not Talk About" (*Pinstripe Fedora*, 2010)
"A Very Bitter Man" (*Los Angeles Times*, 2010)
"Carbon Beach" (*You Don't Have a Clue: Mystery for Teens*, Arte Público Press, 2011)
"Like Rivera and Kahlo" (*La Bloga*, 2011)
"Mamá's Advice" (*PANK*, 2013)
"Pluck" (*Codex Journal*, 2013)
"Bar 107" (*PRISM*, 2014)
"The Last Dream of Pánfilo Velasco" (*Fairy Tale Review*, 2014)
"Still Life with Woman and Stroller" (*Superstition Review*, 2014)
"The Three Mornings of José Antonio Rincón" (*PANK*, 2014)
"Elizondo Returns Home" (*Fourth & Sycamore*, 2015)
"@chicanowriter" (*Fourth & Sycamore*, 2016)
"Gig Economy" (*Los Angeles Review of Books*, 2016)
"Good Things Happen at Tina's Café" (*LA Fiction Anthology: Southland Stories by Southland Writers*, Red Hen Press, 2016)
"The King of Lighting Fixtures" (*Ghost Town Literary Magazine*, 2016)
"Needle" (*Fourth & Sycamore*, 2016)

About the Author

DANIEL A. OLIVAS received his BA in English literature at Stanford University and his law degree at the University of California, Los Angeles. He is currently an attorney with the California Department of Justice in the Public Rights Division. Olivas has written seven books, one of which is the award-winning novel *The Book of Want* (University of Arizona Press, 2011). His works have been published in the *New York Times, El Paso Times, Los Angeles Times, Huffington Post, Los Angeles Review of Books, Jewish Journal*, and many more. He edited the landmark anthology *Latinos in Lotusland* (Bilingual Press, 2008), and co-edited *The Coiled Serpent: Poets Arising from the Cultural Quakes and Shifts of Los Angeles* (Tía Chucha Press, 2016).